DEDICATION

This one is for you Mom. Wish you could have been here to read it.

To Dolly Thank you for being my biggest fan.

To Lee Thank you for always being there and believing

To my Tribe, each day you make me prouder.

To all the students at MKD Karate. Thank you for showing me what an indomitable spirit, compassion, and community look like.

To you the reader
Thank you for joining me on this adventure, ready?

Blur-A John Kane Novel

By Orlando Sanchez

Published by OM Publishing

Copyright 2014 Orlando Sanchez

Other titles by Orlando Sanchez

The Spiritual Warriors

Follow Orlando at

Blog http://nascentnovels.com/

Facebook https://www.facebook.com/OSanchezAuthor

Twitter https://twitter.com/SenseiOrlando

Chapter One

The call came as these calls usually do, in the middle of the night. The phone rang twice before he picked it up. It was four am. He knew, calls at this hour, usually meant one of two things, someone died, or needed to.

"Hello John." He recognized the voice, Trevor.

"Where?"

"Your usual morning haunt. Let's say half past six?" Trevor's accent was still as thick as he remembered. The statement itself was telling. It meant he had been under surveillance for several months. This was not a surprise; he knew they would probably be watching him for the rest of his life. The usual haunt, as Trevor suggested was John's favorite Starbucks. It was located on the corner of 79th street and 37th avenue in Jackson Heights, Queens. John enjoyed his coffee there every morning. It was a routine he enjoyed. Routines, he knew, had a habit of killing people like him, so he took steps to vary the frequency of his visits, picking odd times, occasionally missing a day or two. It was obvious he didn't vary enough.

I must be slipping. He got out of bed and headed to the bathroom.

He got there at six, the barista, Lisa, was just opening up. As Starbucks went, this was one of the most comfortable. It was also the only one in the neighborhood. John's training took over the moment he entered a place. He noticed everything and then put it in the back of his brain. It was automatic and had saved his life on more than one occasion. His brain was doing it now as he sat waiting in the Starbucks. There were two large panes of glass that bookended the entrance to create the face of the shop. Immediately upon entering, on the left was a large square table that sat four.

Along the left wall were four small round tables evenly spaced, two chairs each. On the right side was a long, high backed sofa that threatened to swallow you if you sat on it. Four more of the round tables shared the sofa each with a chair. Further along on the right was a leather sofa, with a low oval table before it.

Surrounding the oval table were three rust colored wingback chairs. Above the sofa were three large mirrors arranged in what may be considered tasteful décor. The counter was next, and this followed the template of most Starbucks: display case followed by cashier station, followed by coffee/espresso/exotic coffee machine area. In the back before the bathrooms there were more of the wingbacks. It made John wonder if there was a sale on the rust colored chairs at some point. The walls were a pale off-white and contrasted with the wood paneling that ran the entire length of shop.

On the walls, in decorative frames, were prints of coffee from different parts of the world. Estate Pacamara from El Salvador rested beside Elephant Kinjia from Africa. Each print portrayed a geographic image of its point of origin. The lighting was dim as usual, an homage to the bistros of yesterday. It was an attempt at atmosphere that succeeded on some basic level. To finish it off, the tile floor accented the wood and contrasted the walls perfectly.

The place was a temple and coffee was its god. And like every place of worship, there was music, music which on the whole gave John a headache. Since he was the only patron at this hour, Lisa mercifully refrained torturing him with the music. She had his coffee, black, waiting at the cashier.

"Thank you Lisa," John said as he paid with a twenty for a two dollar cup of coffee.

He always put the change in the clear plastic tip cube sitting next to the register. He felt it was small price to pay for an hour or so of silence before the morning rush and policy forced Lisa to turn on the music. They were always apologetic when they did turn it on. John would just smile and assure them it was OK. He took his customary chair in the back beside the other wingbacks. His chair provided him with an unobstructed view of the entrance and easy access to the service entrance and bathrooms.

Forget slipping. He sipped his coffee. *This is full blown sloppiness.*

At first glance, the place looked like a deathtrap, two exits easily guarded, which meant easily controlled. John knew different. Inside the staff bathroom, was an unused service door that had been sheet rocked over. A quick look at the plans of the Starbucks confirmed what he suspected. The door led to the restaurant next door, from there to a stairwell that exited behind the restaurant into an alleyway. The exit was out of the line of sight of the building on the northwest corner of 79th Street, a perfect place to position a sniper. The staff bathroom was never used during business hours, which meant it was locked. It cut down on work for AnnMarie, the manager, who only had to maintain the remaining two customer bathrooms. John convinced AnnMarie that he was something of a germaphobe. That, coupled with his large tips, garnered him a key to the staff bathroom that he used sparingly.

At six thirty exactly, a figure strode in to the shop. He was tall, with chiseled features more appropriate on the cover of some men's fashion magazine. Dressed in a dark blue Armani suit, he exuded privilege. Everything about him was impeccable. The hair was perfect, not a strand out of place. The tie, some exotic blue silk, was tied in a perfect Windsor. The shirt, a white which seemed to faintly glow was pressed and starched to perfection. John looked at the figure approaching him, taking in the gait, the calm assured manner in which he moved. He noticed the poise, the economy of motion. The man was highly trained. If it came down to it, he would be difficult to subdue.

Subdue? No he would have to kill if it came to that. Trevor sat in the wingback facing John, his back to the door. It was a clear indicator that he had nothing to fear at this meeting. John knew he would have men stationed at the entrance and service exit. This Starbucks was about to have its slowest morning in history.

"Trevor," said John

He took in the complete image, carefully crafted to disguise the predator lying beneath the surface of polish and fashion. Trevor settled into this chair placing his Halliburton case beside him. He crossed his legs, the Bruno Magli on his feet screamed excess and vanity. It was all a sham, a façade that John saw through.

"Hello John, we need to talk." The words were fast and clipped.

Something has him worried, thought John.

"I'm here, talk."

"Direct as always. I always appreciated that about you John."

"I'm only here, because it's you, Trevor."

Trevor held up his hand as he reached for the case. John tensed slightly. Trevor deliberately slowed his hand, and pulled out a CD case, placing it on the table along with a file folder.

"Tell me John, have you had any new students?"

"No."

"Are you certain?" Trevor said as he pushed the file on the table followed by the disc closer to John.

6

"You came all this way to ask me a question, I'm sure you know the answer to. Why?"

"I needed to make sure, see your eyes. I remember Kei fondly as well." said Trevor.

The name struck a chord, not a day passed that he didn't think about her.

John looked away. "What do you want Trevor."

"Someone is eliminating our assets," said Trevor.

"And this is my concern how?"

"Whoever is doing this is very skilled, trained by the best."

"Sounds like an internal matter to me, why call me?" said John.

"We put some of our best on apprehending the target; none of our people came back."

"What aren't you telling me Trevor?"

For the first time John saw Trevor's composure slip.

"This person can blur," said Trevor, looking directly into John's eyes.

"Impossible." said John.

"We all thought so." said Trevor.

In a subdued voice John said almost to himself. "I was Nakamura Sensei's last student. I only taught Kei and I saw her die. Your people are wrong. It's clear you're mistaken."

"You can see now why I am here. If it's not you or someone you trained. Then we have a serious situation on our hands. We need you to secure the target, John. You're probably the only one who can." said Trevor slowly.

Trevor pointed at the file and disc.

"Everything we know is on that disc and in that folder. Call me after you review it." said Trevor.

Trevor stood to leave, dusting off his sleeve as he did so.

"I really hope we are wrong about this John, maybe it's like you said an internal matter. I don't need to tell you the natural progression of things if this person isn't stopped."

The words hung in the air.

John knew what Trevor meant. If the target wasn't stopped, he would factor high on the threat list; this meeting was a warning, a not so veiled threat, as it was a mission. Someone had to be held accountable and he fit the bill. John picked up the file and disc.

"I'll give you a call later." said John.

Trevor turned and headed to the door. Speaking into the hidden microphone embedded in his collar button. "He has the file, let's see what he comes up with. Give him some room to move but stay close."

Trevor turned at the door and looked back at John, knowing the next time they met it could be as enemies.

Chapter Two

John grabbed the file and disc. He waited a moment for Trevor's squad to leave the front of Starbucks, fully aware that a shadow group would be left behind to monitor his movements. He decided he would stay and wait for the post office across the street to open. It would be a two hour wait which gave him plenty of time to review the file.

The first few pages were the usual- mission objectives, targets and locations. It wasn't until the fourth page that it got interesting. Each time a target was to be eliminated, the asset met with a confrontation. In each case, and John counted five, each confrontation was fatal for the asset. He could understand one or two, but five? It was too many to be coincidence. John didn't believe in coincidences.

"Lisa, can I use your phone?" said John.

"Sure John, you know where it is."

She pointed to the back with her chin. It wasn't that John was a Luddite; he usually avoided carrying a cell phone and didn't own a computer because he knew the tracking potential they posed. In his younger days he was an accomplished code breaker, and visited his local FedEx Kinkos on a regular basis to keep his keyboard skills sharp.

John dialed a number; it took a minute before it rang. If they were tracing this call, they would see that he was calling Central Queens, when in reality; even he didn't know where he was calling. All he knew was that he was calling the best.

"Hello John, are you still drinking that slop water they call coffee? Switch to tea, man, tea." John smiled.

"Hello Mole. I have a disc I need you to take a look at."

Mole's real name was Peter Cheung. He had been top of his class at M.I.T. when he graduated. An intuitive genius with anything technological, he was recruited right out of school and worked for Eclipse International for three years before he got too curious. Peter being Peter dug a little too deeply into his employer's infrastructure. He was discovered and it was determined, he should take an early retirement.

The job was given to John, who for the first time, rather than eliminate a target, saved one. It was right after losing Kei, and he knew then his days were numbered as an asset. He had saved Peter, staged his death and with Peter's help erased any trace that Peter ever existed. He also gave Peter explicit instructions that would keep him alive as well as enough money to keep him comfortable and equipped with his latest gadgetry, Peter didn't become the best by being sloppy. He was as formless as vapor and managed to stay under the radar

9

and off the grid. Only John had a direct way of contacting him, a number that was routed through so many hubs it would take ten years to successfully trace it beyond the surface location of Central Queens. If they ever decided to follow the trace, it would lead them to a public telephone kiosk that ironically, had no telephone. Peter had gone underground and disappeared, becoming the Mole.

"What kind of disc is it?" asked Mole.

"Proof of something." said John.

"Proof of what?" said Mole

"That's the question of the hour." said John

Chapter Three

"Sure John, I'll take a look at it. Are you near a computer?" asked Mole.

"Not yet, but I will be in –" John looked at his watch, an old Timex chronograph that kept perfect time, "ninety minutes. I just have to make one stop first."

"Ok John, you remember the procedure?"

"I'm not quite that old, Mole," said John.

"Old enough grandpa, I'll speak to you later."

And with that, Mole hung up. The entire conversation took fifteen seconds. John could see the sun creeping over the rooftops. It was going to be a sunny day. The few morning clouds would be burned away by mid-morning giving way to a bright summer day.

John headed back into the main area of the Starbucks.

"Thank you Lisa," he said.

"Anytime John," she answered.

Scrapping the post office idea, he decided he would head back home and walk the dog before he saw what was on the disc.

"Leaving early today?" said Lisa.

"Have a few errands to run, plus the dog gets cranky if I don't get him out early."

Lisa smiled and John gave her a wave as he stepped out of the Starbucks. The baristas flirted with him shamelessly because they knew he would never take them seriously. He was old enough to be her father. He walked along 37th Avenue, heading towards 85th Street. Most of the stores along the avenue were still closed this early in the morning. In two hours the avenue would be full of patrons and people walking to the 82nd Street train station, to begin their morning commute. John really enjoyed Jackson Heights.

It was a diverse neighborhood that mixed in a bit of every culture. From 75th St. down was Little India, where you could find most things Indian or South Asian. Between 75th and 95th, it was a mix of Latino, Jewish, and American culture, meshing and vying for expression in every way, from restaurants to community centers. It was no accident John had retired here at the ripe old age of thirty-five, which was old, considering his profession.

No, he had moved here because his roots were in Jackson Heights. After being nomadic for so long, it felt good to put down roots somewhere. He also knew the inherent danger in being rooted, and was prepared to vanish if the occasion required it.

On 85th Street, he turned left off 37th Avenue, heading to the residential area of 34th and 35th Avenues. His house, a corner lot on 85th and 34th Avenue was a detached Victorian. His entire block was landmarked as were many of the homes in Jackson Heights, which meant he could not alter the façade of the house without extensive paperwork, and even then it could be denied. He liked that aspect of his neighborhood, the old world feeling in the midst of the modern, the clash of old and new.

As he opened his door, he made his way to security panel, lifted the false keyboard and pressed his thumb into the screen. It was an alarm he installed, if tripped it would release an odorless and colorless gas, very much like carbon monoxide, without the fatal side effects. In a few minutes, any would-be intruder would be unconscious, unaware of what was happening. As John made his way to the living room, his dog, Storm padded over. Rescued by the North Shore Animal League, he picked him up as a pup. For a German shepherd, he was on the large side. He looked more wolf than dog and John felt that somewhere, Storm felt closer to being a wolf as well.

They had an understanding. It wasn't so much that John picked him but that they picked each other. Storm unlike other dogs did not jump up to greet his master but rather waited patiently for him to enter the house before he would pad over silently, and acknowledge John. If John had to describe the dog in on one word, it would be stoic. John grabbed the leash, even though he never used it, the leash was a signal, a routine they had developed. John would grab the leash and Storm would head to the door. John enjoyed walking with Storm; he felt a deep kinship with the animal. Sometimes it was easier to relate to animals than people. At least it was simpler. You always knew where you stood with an animal; guile was something relegated to people. John preferred dealing with animals. He walked around the block several times, allowing the surveillance teams to see him before he headed inside.

The walks allowed him to think or solve tricky problems, while having Storm as an alert companion. It was one of the few times he could let his guard down partially. He walked back inside. Storm trailing behind him, and headed to the basement. He picked up the devices Mole made for him and walked to the nearest Fedex Kinkos store, located on 82nd Street and Northern Blvd. It was a 24 hour location which made more sense for the Kinkos side of the establishment than the Fedex. John couldn't see the need in shipping something at 3am, but he was sure someone did. He walked to the counter and waited, he knew Jerry the night manager played video games at night on his laptop and it usually took a while for him to realize there was someone at the front counter. Business would pick up in an hour or so and Jerry would be relieved of his shift. After a few minutes Jerry came to the front.

"Morning John," he said, through a yawn.

"Good morning Jerry. How is everything in the virtual world?"

"On a kick ass task force that is making me reconsider online gaming. Six hours and we just finished. These pugs are killing me." said Jerry.

John nodded as if he understood half of what Jerry was saying.

"I need a computer, one in the back, please." said John.

"Sure thing, you can have that one over there" Jerry said, as he pointed to a computer in the back corner. "Number seven, it's kind of private."

John paid for an hour and thanked Jerry. He sat in front of the machine; the flat screen took up little space. John remembered when monitors were huge affairs, boxes that took up all of the desk space. He took out the glasses case he carried. In it was a pair of non-prescription glasses that looked like reading glasses, in a compartment behind the glasses were the devices Mole made for him. They looked like the remote receivers for a wireless mouse. He plugged them both in to the USB ports provided and waited. One was an ISP scrambler that allowed John to access sensitive material from any computer without it being traced back to the computer he was on. The other was a hard disk bypass, effectively erasing the presence of John every five seconds.

John called Mole from his throwaway cell, punching in the sequence of numbers that would let Mole know he was at the computer. The ISP scrambler also allowed Mole the ability to track John and speak with him via computer, a much faster and smoother version of Skype. An avatar appeared on the screen. Justice blindfolded. In her hands instead of scales, she held an AK47. John smiled.

"Hello John." the words flashed in the text box.

"Hello Mole, are you ready? I think the disc probably has some tracing program so find ED."

ED wasn't a person but meant extremely dangerous and potentially life threatening.

"ED is close by. I will keep him on standby in case he needs to step in." said Mole.

"Inserting disc." said John as he placed the CD in the reader.

"More than just a trace program, but not an issue for ED."

There was a brief pause then the text flew on to the screen.

"Oh shit, you need to see this then get out of there, fast." said Mole.

John pulled the keyboard closer and his fingers sped over the keys of their own accord.

"OK I bought myself a little time, Mole. What's up?" said John.

There was a pause. "Elegant grandpa, but it won't fake them out long." said Mole.

John had launched a program that would send burst transmissions from different network hubs every ten seconds. It was a virtual goose chase.

"Long enough, what's on the disc?" said John.

A window opened and then enlarged to fill the screen. The screen was black for a moment then showed the perspective of a street corner.

"Mole find out where this was taken." said John.

"Already on it, looks like Upper west side, 96th St. and Columbus."

"I didn't realize there were cameras on that corner." said John.

"Oh this isn't your regular run of the mill NYPD camera install. This is more along the lines of Hello 1984, welcome home George Orwell type of tech. These cameras are installed in the lights."

"Which lights?"

"You know, red means stop, green means go." said Mole.

"In the lights?" said John.

The screen suddenly came to life; John could tell it was early evening. Mole was right; the picture quality surpassed everything he had seen out there except maybe Eclipse or Consortium level tech.

"Can you tell who made the tech, it's too good to be military or even black ops."

"Give me a day or two and I will find out who the little bugger is that made this." said Mole.

The image panned left then right. John looked at the counter on the computer screen next to the image. He had fifteen minutes before he had to disconnect. Fortunately there were only eight minutes left on the disc. It was going to be close with a seven minute window. The image panned right and stopped. John was impressed as the image zoomed in on a face and showed the telltale signs of face recognition software.

"Face recog?" John asked Mole.

"Down to the last pimple, this blows away anything overseas. Whoever this is, they are heavily funded. This isn't supposed to be available at this level for another five years," said Mole.

John didn't recognize the face even though the software did. The name came up as Adam Brown. John knew it was an alias. Adam had that everyman type of face, non-descript, average, average height, average build. The perfect type of asset was the one that could blend into a crowd easily and be forgotten.

Suddenly a figure appeared next to Adam much to his surprise, which was considerable given that it registered on his face and he was a trained asset. The figure's face was covered by a baseball cap as if he or she knew of the camera's existence.

"Male or female, Mole?" said John.

"I can't tell I'm going for very thin male or very strong female." said Mole.

The figure stood next to Adam and said something into his ear.

"Mole." said John.

"On it, the mystery figure is saying... This is not personal."

"What isn't personal?" thought John.

Adam turned to strike the figure when it seemed for a brief moment the disc skipped some seconds. John looked at the counter, nothing had skipped. He moved the cursor back a few seconds just to make sure.

"John, what the hell was that? Did I just not see what I saw?"

A few seconds later, Adam fell crumpled to the ground. He was dead before he hit the floor. John knew what had happened. He just couldn't believe it.

"Mole, it's time to go. I will contact you later for the manufacturer of the camera." said John.

"Sure thing." said Mole subdued. "John this is not good. I know that isn't you, but –"

"Later." said John. He packed his things, removed the bypass and ISP scrambler. He looked around making sure he was alone.

John knew where Mole was going, he had just witnessed someone use a technique that was known only to him. He replayed the few seconds once again, conscious of the timer counting down.

There was no doubt, the mystery figure could blur.

John had about three minutes to exit the Fedex Kinkos. It gave him enough time to thank Jerry and walk out the door. As he made his way to the sidewalk, two cars pulled up silently. John now far enough away to watch, saw the three men and one woman get out in a measured pace. He could tell from the way the men waited for the woman that she was running this group.

John managed to take her picture with the phone and send it to Mole. Then he broke the phone into its component pieces making sure to remove any type of SIM card and throwing the pieces of the phone down the sewer grating.

The group entered the Fedex Kinkos with practiced ease, this was a federal or anti cyber terrorist squad. They were highly trained, which concerned John.

Who would mobilize that fast?

More importantly who had the technical muscle to track him, despite his precautions? This didn't feel like Trevor. He needed to make some calls after he found out who the woman was.

Chapter Four

Mikaela Petrovich entered the Fedex Kinkos with her team. She stood at the counter with measured poise while her team fanned out beside her. She waited patiently for an entire minute, before indicating to Gustav, with a nod that she wanted to speak to someone. Gustav had been with her the longest. They understood each other and she rarely had to give him verbal instructions. Gustav stood six foot two inches, and tipped the scale at two hundred and forty pounds. He was a giant compared to Mikaela's five foot stature. In moments a startled Jerry appeared from the back office with Gustav trailing behind. Mikaela had the gift of a photographic memory. She scanned her memory for a moment to see if Jerry was somehow relevant to her, and decided he wasn't.

"Hello, Jerry is it?" she said as she read the name tag.

"Yeah, how can I help you?" he answered looking warily at the two men beside Mikaela.

"There was a person using a terminal in this location exactly," she looked at her watch, "ten minutes ago." Jerry looked around to terminal seven where John no longer was. He decided it was in his best interest to cooperate.

"Yeah, there's a guy who comes every so often. He was on terminal seven."

Mikaela motioned to the two men beside her and they made their way to the terminal. Once there, they began to dismantle and remove the terminal.

"Hey! You guys can't do that! I'm responsible for it if something happens!" yelled Jerry.

Mikaela stood quietly observing her team.

"I understand and I don't want to cause you unnecessary problems. Have your supervisor call me when he gets in." she said.

She handed Jerry a business card. Embossed on it was her name, M. Petrovich and a direct number. The two men walked out with the terminal. Gustav stepped around the counter to stand beside Mikaela.

"This is a matter of national security, Jerry. We appreciate your cooperation," said Mikaela.

"Yeah sure," he said as he looked down at the card Mikaela had given him. Mikaela turned with Gustav behind her. When she stepped outside the Fedex Kinkos, she paused and scanned the street and adjacent sidewalk. Across the street was a figure whose face was obscured by the brim of a baseball cap looking her way. For a brief moment the figure turned and Mikaela was able to see part of the face clearly. She filed that away in her memory in case it was relevant.

Chapter Five

John made his way to another mobile phone outlet a few blocks away. They were cropping up all over these days. He bought two pay as you go cell phones and activated one. He put in a SIM card that created a scrambled signal. It was another one of Mole's devices. He punched in a sequence of numbers that connected him to Mole.

"Hey there John, using the scrambler, excellent." said Mole.

"Remember, old not stupid, at least not yet." said John.

"Got it, the photo you sent over with your craptastic camera phone took a while."

"Were you able to find out who she is?"

"I said your phone was craptastic. My stuff on the other hand is phenomenal." said Mole.

"Congratulations. Do we have a name?"

"Thank you. Her name is Mikaela Petrovich."

"Who does she work for, who has that kind of response time?"

"That's the interesting part; she doesn't exist, at least not officially." said Mole.

John expected that, so her official black status didn't surprise him.

"Is she part of the alphabet soup?" said John.

John was referring to the numerous three letter government agencies that contained covert operatives.

"Doesn't look like it. Plus Uncle Sam is probably still trying to unscramble the signal. These people were there inside fifteen minutes, scary fast." said Mole.

John thought for a moment.

"If this isn't government maybe it's a private contractor, could it be Eclipse?" said John.

"Not their M.O. Plus why would they be interested in you?" said Mole.

"Find out who she is and who she works for. I don't like the fact that they got here so fast." said John.

"I'll get on it." said Mole.

It was a good point, John had never done any work officially for Eclipse International, the contract he violated was through a third party broker and was untraceable back to him, he made sure of that. It was also unlikely they knew what was on the disc.

"I found something hold on a sec." said Mole.

John could hear the keystrokes that meant Mole was processing information.

"It's encrypted to hell but it could be worth checking out." said Mole.

"What is it?" said John.

"It's a company name and address. Double Helix, the address is 65 Crescent Street, near the Queensboro Bridge in Long Island City. I don't think it's related to your guests. This came over in a transmission while you were on the computer. This is some badass work John." said Mole.

John knew the area. It was an industrial park located in West Queens, when some large corporations saw the edge of Queens as a promising location to place some of their facilities. In its heyday, about twenty five years earlier, it was a thriving area. Now it was mostly deserted, especially at night.

"This smells like a trap John, at the very least a dangerous clue. The encryption was weird, specific yet vague, like a test. I don't like it. That transmission probably caused the visit." said Mole.

John had learned early on to trust Mole on matters such as these. He still had to go.

"Duly noted, I will be extra careful Mole."

"Well, don't go jumping through hoops for me."

John smiled. He knew it was Mole's way of showing concern.

"I will connect when I get there."

"Ok, don't get dead," answered Mole and hung up.

Chapter Six

Long Island City had changed considerably since John last visited. What used to be primordially an industrial area, factories and offices was trying its hardest to transform into an up and coming residential neighborhood. Getting there was easy, John took the 7 train headed to Manhattan and got off at Queensboro Plaza. He was careful to change his route enough to lose any obvious tail, knowing that the possibility of surveillance still existed. He wasn't really concerned about it. Trevor would be watching, he proceeded as if this were the default state and acted accordingly.

Crescent Street was one of those key streets that intersected into the plaza. During the day it was congested with traffic heading into Manhattan via the 59th Street Bridge. Now however at 7pm, it was mostly deserted, with traffic heading into Queens mostly.

65 Crescent Street was a new addition to the neighborhood. As far as the area went, it was small and nondescript. Standing four stories, it seemed like a displaced brownstone from the Upper East Side of Manhattan and looked out of place in this neighborhood. The only feature that set it apart from its neighbors was the smoked glass façade.

That façade didn't come cheap. He walked up to the entrance, figuring the direct approach was best. The door was plain with no distinguishing features. It was also heavy and secure. John could tell the owners took their privacy seriously. Above the door was a camera, it angled to take in the entire doorway and some of the street. To the right of the doorway sat a small glass panel roughly eight inches by eight inches. John's internal alarms, while not fully set off were on edge. Something was off about this whole situation. If he were honest he could trace this feeling of unease to the moment he viewed the footage on the disc.

He knew rationally that what he saw should not have been possible. Nakamura Sensei was a stern and unforgiving teacher. The fact that he accepted John as a student was a matter of John's potential and some other hidden reason he never shared. Nakamura Sensei, even with his abrasive manner, had no lack of people waiting to train under him. He would interview prospective students, one or two a year, and was unrelentingly brutal. Many failed his grueling training in the first month. Tall for an Asian, standing at five foot eleven, he was thin and wiry. He moved with an easy grace that belied his amazing speed and incredible strength. His hair was always cut short and he was always dressed impeccably and more often than not in traditional garments. His features were typically Asian, and his eyes held an intensity that burned into you. His English, like his Japanese, French, Spanish and Italian were flawless.

John always wondered about the languages Nakamura Sensei knew. He asked him once, the answer, given tersely, was to focus on his training not languages.

Given Sensei's disposition would he have trained another in the okuden – the hidden techniques of his family's art? John couldn't see it. The problem with that scenario is that it left John as the only one with the ability to erase assets. Even though he didn't have motive, he had plenty of opportunity. Trevor's warning was clear: find who was doing the killing or become the one implicated. He took out his phone and called Mole.

"Hello John, how does it look?" said Mole.

"It doesn't. This place is pretty secure. Take a look."

John took a picture of the front of the building with his phone and sent it to Mole.

"Seriously John, do you even plan on investing in a real phone with a semi decent camera?"

"It's on my to do list Mole. What do you think?" said John.

"Well that doesn't look inviting. Are you sure it's the right address? I know how you senior citizens get things mixed up. You aren't at 56 Crescent, right?" said Mole.

John let that one go, knowing his silence would answer.

"Ok, ok. Let me see here. You see that panel on the right? It's a handprint reader. That's the lock. The door is on a pneumatic release. If you have the right print, you have access." said Mole.

"Isn't this a bit sophisticated; I mean we're in Queens, not Langley." said John.

"Not anymore it isn't but it does say something about whomever these people are, they like their privacy." John agreed.

"What's the plan? No way can I hack that interface even if I were there next to you." said Mole.

"I know, only one thing to try." said John.

John placed his right hand on the glass panel. An imprint of his hand remained on the panel in a blue fluorescent after image. It was quickly followed by the image of a DNA strand. The symbolism was not lost on John, a double helix.

There was a shifting of mechanisms on the other side of the door followed by a low hiss. The door swung inward.

"Well, color me embarrassed, it looks like someone is expecting you John." said Mole.

"Looks that way." said John. *How did they get his handprint?*

"I don't like it John, but I know that's not going to prevent you from going into the bat cave, is it?"

"Too many questions now Mole, questions that need answers. See if you can find out who runs Double Helix or who owns this property." said John.

"Fine, you see the glass on the fascia? It has an electro static charge, no cell phones, bugs tracers or any electronic devices that aren't keyed to the building." Mole sounded impressed.

"Sounds like you're a fan." said John.

"Shit John, I can appreciate beauty man, and that, is beautiful. It also means once you go in I can't reach you. " said Mole.

"I'm going in blind."

"Exactly, so maybe you want some back up? I can get one of the guys over there in twenty."

"No, if it's nothing, then it's a wasted trip, and if it's dangerous, they become a liability. If I'm not out in an hour, set the backup plan in motion." said John.

"You sure?" said Mole.

"One hour Mole, from now." said John.

Mole heard the edge in John's voice and knew better than to argue. John stepped inside, the door closed silently behind him; the locking mechanism slid into place, trapping him inside.

The hallway was cool and dim. A few feet on his right was the opening to a large living room. John stood still to let his eyes adjust to the lower light level. The floors were hardwood. John could see that much. There were prints or photos of some sort lining the hallway but he couldn't make them out. Most of the furniture was low in a traditional Japanese style. Something about the place made him feel comfortable and welcome. John sensed the presence before he saw him.

"Good evening Kane-san," he pronounced John's name with two syllables Kah-neh. John turned slowly not because he was afraid, but rather the sheer physical presence the man was radiating was intimidating. He had not felt that kind of physical energy since his Sensei.

John turned to face an old man advanced in years.

"Ninety five, next week." the old man said reading the question on John's face.

"Do I know you?" said John.

The old man moved gracefully, despite his age and settled on one of the cushions beside the table.

"Please sit. To answer your question, no, you do not know me, but I have been waiting for you. You may know of me or rather of my exploits." said the old man.

John scrutinized the old man sitting before him so serenely.

"I'm sorry. I don't know you." said John after a few moments.

"It's quite all right; it has been a long time. When I was young I had many names. My family name is Fujita. My given name was, or rather is, although very few alive remember it, Takashi."

Realization dawned on John's face.

"When I was young and full of energy, I went by a different name." said the old man.

"The Katana." whispered John.

The old man bowed his head slightly.

"Would you like some tea? We have much to discuss." said Fujita.

John sat down in a state of semi-shock. The man before him was a living piece of history. John thought back to the stories of the Fujita clan Nakamura Sensei shared with him. The Fujita clan was one of the driving forces throughout the history of Japan dating as far back as the early 1300s. The clan preferred to blend in and remain behind the scenes, careful to remain hidden and undiscovered. The few exceptions to this were the near mystical swordsmen the Fujita clan had produced. Above them all stood Takashi Fujita. Known as the Katana, it was said he could strike down an opponent between blinks. That he had trained his body to such a degree that he was impervious to sword cuts, even bullets.

John sat and stared. Fujita's body was gnarled by years of training. He realized he was being rude and quickly lowered his eyes. He was so transfixed by the old man that he didn't notice the woman approaching beside him.

John was at a loss, the fact that he was meeting a revered budoka, and that it was his own handprint that opened the lock to this home conspired to unsettle him, he lashed out in reflex at the woman that had silently sidled up to him unseen until that moment.

The woman carried a tray with fine china on it; she deftly ducked out of the way of his strike and continued her motions placing the tray on the table. She bowed and poured tea for the two men. Her face, serene as she poured the tea gave John the impression she thought upon other matters. When she finished, she bowed and stepped behind Fujita, sitting gracefully behind him and slightly to his right in a kneeling position called seiza. Her eyes appeared to be closed, but John couldn't be sure. He couldn't guess her age; she had a timeless quality about her. She wore a simple black kimono, her hair, which was loose, hung straight framing her face.

"This is Masami," Fujita gestured to the woman. "I rescued her when she was a young girl and about to lose her life. She has since pledged her life to me, and to my clan."

John looked at Masami, who despite the scrutiny remained motionless.

"She is here to take care of me in my final days which draw close. I am sure you have several questions. I will try to answer them all to the best of my ability." said Fujita.

John felt like he had stepped into some strange world, there was no way he could be having a Q&A with one of Japan's living legends. Yet here he was, and there he was as real as the air he breathed.

John took a deep breath and gathered his wits.

"This is going to take more than an hour, I need to make a call, is that possible?" asked John.

Masami stood in response to the almost imperceptible nod from Fujita. She left the room and returned to the room minutes later. As she sat, Fujita gestured to John. "Your phone should be operational now."

John removed his phone from his pocket and sure enough he had a signal. Before he dialed, he bowed to Fujita.

"If I may?" said John.

Fujita returned to bow, "Please attend to your matter."

John called Mole.

"John! Is that you?" said Mole.

Mole was nervous or he never would have asked.

"Mole forget the backup plan, I'm calling you from the inside."

"No way, your signal shows you clear across town, are you sure you're inside?" said Mole incredulous.

"Yes Mole, I'm pretty certain I'm inside sitting down at a table across from one of the last people I ever expected to see."

"Who?" asked Mole.

John inclined his head, asking Fujita if he could share this information. Fujita nodded.

"I'm sitting across from Fujita Sensei, Takashi Fujita."

After the clacking of some keys, John heard Mole whistle low and long.

"John." said Mole. "Are you sure you're cool man?"

"I'm fine Mole, a bit shocked but good." said John.

"If that's the Fujita Sensei, dude, he was awesome! Also says here he's dead. Dead ten years in fact. Either you're right or you're sitting with a ghost. One other thing, whatever is scrambling your signal is off the charts, better than anything I could do, watch your back." said Mole.

"Will do, thanks Mole." said John.

"Oh! One more thing." said Mole.

"What, Mole?"

"Get me an autograph, or maybe a sword he used? Maybe an old sweat rag Maybe a-"

"Goodbye Mole." said John.

He cut off Mole mid-sentence and put the phone away. The call averted the sanitizing of his home and Mole erasing all pertinent data on him. It was an extreme course of action, but one set in place from years of experience.

"My apologies, Fujita Sensei." said John.

"None required. Let us go to the drawing room where we can converse and discuss your visit here and what it means to those who seek you harm." said Fujita.

Chapter Seven

Fujita Sensei stood with a grace that belied his years. Masami stood silently after him. Fujita Sensei led the way to a room of a more intimate nature. This was a room that said close friends and family. The furniture was solid and dark wood, but the arrangement was inviting, informal and open. More cushions were spread around the floor. The room was spacious with one wall being shoji screens. The screens were partially open and John could see what looked like a Zen garden beyond the screen doors. Fujita Sensei sat on one of the cushions. Masami left the room after bowing to the older man. John sat on one of the cushions opposite Fujita; memories of his training flooded him. After a moment John spoke.

"I guess the most obvious question is, why am I here and how did I open that door?" said John.

"That is two questions. These questions will inevitably lead to more questions, but it's a start." said Fujita.

"Let's start there." said John

Fujita Sensei took a sip from his tea, as if to gather his thoughts. The smell of honey and mint filled the air.

"Very well, you are here because your associate Peter Cheung discovered an encryption on a disc that was given to you by your former colleagues. These same colleagues wish you to ascertain the identity of an unknown individual who possesses a specific ability; it is the same ability that you possess. You are also here because despite the evidence on that disc, you are the last legitimate student of Nakamura Sensei, and as such the inheritor of his estate. You were able to open the door because your print is one of a handful allowed onto this property, property that belongs to your late sensei." said Fujita in a calm voice.

John remained silent, but didn't let the shock of the revelation register on his face.

"That- that was pretty accurate." said John.

"As you may know, my family has been in the shadows for centuries, shaping entire governments. Tracking one man, even one as formidable as you, was not a difficult task. You will find that the Double Helix Corp. is a subsidiary of Fujita International. The Fujita conglomerate of companies is a legitimate body of organizations. Only those of the bloodline are allowed to become aware of the hidden nature of the parent company."

"How many of the Fujita clan still live?" said John.

Fujita Sensei smiled, "Fortunately many of my brethren believed in expanding the family tree. We are very numerous, even though many have taken on other names to better blend in with their environment."

"How did you do that with the disc?" said John.

"It wasn't on the disc. We placed the encryption on the terminal when you were sending information to your computer friend. That action triggered the visit by

30

government computer police, not that they will find anything on the machine." said Fujita.

"But how did you know which terminal I was using?"

"That part was simple; we simply had a person watching from a vantage point with an unobstructed view of the establishment."

"What if I had gone to another Fedex?" asked John.

"Why would you? This was the one you went to regularly, and we are creatures of habit, as you know." said Fujita.

John hated that he was right, and that he had been so easy to track. He was getting soft and slow, he could afford neither.

"The information Mo- Peter discovered led me here. I'm guessing that was the purpose?"

"Correct, Kane-san. I am an old man. Very soon I will be gone. Before I go, I must attend to several matters. You are chief among them."

"Why me?" said John.

Fujita Sensei paused to sip some more tea.

"Your Sensei was one of my best students. We did not always agree, but there was always respect and 'on'-obligation. I disagreed strongly with his choice to work for an organization other than my family. I disagreed but understood that it was his path. This property and all its contents now belong to you. They are a result of his being an operative. He left it to you as his last request."

"He never told me." said John.

"Perhaps he had closed that chapter of his life. Or knowing the path that lay before you, he chose to prepare you as best he could." said Fujita.

"I don't understand. How is this supposed to help me with what's on that disc?" said John.

The old man held up one hand, using a napkin as he coughed for close to twenty seconds. When he removed the napkin from his mouth, John saw traces of blood.

"Time, it is the one enemy that can never be defeated. As you can see, mine is limited. Please allow me to finish."

"My apologies Sensei please continue."

"The ability you possess, the ability taught to your Sensei by my family is only one of five."

"Five?" said John.

It never occurred to him that there were other abilities in existence. It was something his sensei never discussed. He suspected others but could never confirm their existence.

"The five heads of my family each developed ability. How it was done has been lost to time. There was one law in my family; no one other than the leaders of the families could have more than one skill. I'm sure you could understand the reasoning behind this." said Fujita.

John could see the reason clearly. If one person possessed even two abilities, similar to his, that person could be, would be unstoppable.

"What are these abilities?" asked John.

"What I am sharing with you now, is not known to anyone else besides the most eldest of the clan and those of the bloodline. Even then, that information will be incomplete and erroneous to deter those who would pursue power and dominion. Masami will be able to educate you further in time. I will leave you in her care." said Fujita.

"You will what?" John thought he misheard. The old man smiled at John's reaction.

"Do not be alarmed. I have asked her and she has agreed to look after you." said Fujita.

John didn't know how he felt about a baby sitter. He shelved the thought for now.

"Never mind that now." Fujita Sensei said with a wave of his hand as if waving the topic away.

"Let's discuss the abilities of the Five."

"The abilities may seem distinct and unrelated on the surface, but they are deeply connected. The relation of each is a form without a form." said Fujita.

"Excuse me Sensei, that last part about form. I've heard it several times before from Nakamura Sensei. I just couldn't understand what he meant by it."

"I cannot explain it to you Kane-san, it is an answer you must arrive at, I can only point you in the direction."

"With the abilities." said John.

"Precisely, let's start with your ability for example. As I understand it, you and your colleagues called it blurring. Correct?"

"Yes, the ability to move beyond the perception of an opponent." said John.

Fujita Sensei nodded his head and drank some more tea.

"Are you really moving faster? What is your perception of the ability?"

"I don't really feel like I'm moving any faster." said John.

"What would happen if instead of your moving faster, what was really happening was that everyone around you moved slower?" said Fujita.

John thought about that a moment.

"But that would mean –" realization dawned on John's face.

"I can see you are starting to see. Let's get back to that and Kaneko, the founder of your ability, later. The next ability is transforming your skin into a stone-like substance, resistant to all types of damage."

"I could see how that would come in handy." said John.

"Mura who discovered this ability was said to be able to deflect knives and spears with his body, when he executed his ability. However it was very taxing on his system."

"How so?" said John.

"He could only maintain the state for short periods of time, during which he was quite difficult to injure." said Fujita.

"He needed downtime, rest afterwards though?" said John.

"Yes, as you may have surmised, every one of the abilities requires a period of rest equivalent to the duration of time spent using the ability."

"Or else the body shuts down like it or not." said John

Fujita Sensei nodded.

"The body and more importantly, the mind will protect itself, if you don't rest, it will force it upon you. That is one of the fail safes of the abilities, it seems." said Fujita.

John understood the implication.

"If you could use your ability without ever needing to rest, you would be undefeatable." said John.

"True, at least until your early death," said Fujita Sensei.

"That is quite the downside." said John.

Fujita Sensei sipped more tea. His movements were fluid and graceful. John would have liked to see him when he was a young man full of energy.

"I was foolish and full of ego when I was younger." Fujita Sensei said as if reading his mind. "This is why I never respected the next ability, until it saved my life."

"When was this?" John asked clearly intrigued who or what could have endangered the life of this great swordsman.

Waving his hand again Fujita dismissed the question.

"That is a story for another time. The ability that saved me was discovered by Mariko, and I do believe it was Mariko herself who placed hands on me. The practitioners of her ability can heal or accelerate healing or death with a touch-direct or indirect." said Fujita.

"How severe a wound?" said John.

"I saw many brought back from the brink of death. There was even rumored a technique called a life exchange, though I never witnessed it. A person could be brought back from a recent death, provided the practitioner gives up their life." said Fujita.

"That sounds like the Death Hand just the opposite." said John.

"It flows from the same place, giving life and taking it are two sides of the same coin." said Fujita.

"How could it have been Mariko who placed her hands on you?" said John.

"Consider that out of all the abilities, that one could extend life the longest, healing cells on a continual basis, not actively, but almost as a byproduct of use." said Fujita.

"I see, every time she or anyone with this ability used it, they would have the side effect of self-healing, like anti-aging." said John.

Sensei Fujita nodded.

John remained silent a moment, thinking about several people he knew personally who never seemed to age.

"That explains a lot actually," said John.

"I am certain that it does. That is also Masami's ability and I have a feeling it will serve you well in the future as it has me."

That explained Fujita Sensei's advanced age despite his illness.

"The illness you have, Sensei?" asked John.

"Cannot be reversed by Masami, it can only be kept at bay for so long." He sipped some more tea.

"The next ability is one of the most difficult to stand against." said Fujita.

"Why? I would think the others you have mentioned would be quite a challenge."

"Imagine an ability that, once you have shown what you can do, can counter you flawlessly?" said Fujita.

"That would certainly pose a problem." said John.

"It is the ability of mirroring. To a limited degree, this practitioner can mimic any ability, any technique, any fighting style it's exposed to after seeing it once."

"That's all it takes? Seeing it once?" said John.

"Yes. This does not mean the practitioner can execute with the same flawless ability as someone who has been training their entire life. If the practitioner lacks the conditioning, they will be severely limited. What this ability does is impart the understanding and counters to whatever it faces. It is quite formidable to see in action." said Fujita.

"How would you combat something like that?" asked John.

"I hope you never have to find out Kane-san, truly. My advice would be not to be who I am." said Fujita.

"Be someone else?" asked John not quite understanding.

"Exactly, Then at the right moment, be yourself. The next ability is the most fearsome of the five and it is the one most shrouded in mystery.

"Let me guess, invisibility?" said John.

Fujita Sensei looked at John for a long moment before responding.

"Thirty years ago that remark would have earned you much pain. I have since mellowed with age, and you have been watching too many movies." said Fujita.

John remained silent, embarrassed at his levity.

"You have heard of Death touch arts?" asked Fujita Sensei.

"Sure. Dim Mak and the like, yes."

"The last ability is where those distorted versions derive from. The last ability is the death touch."

"Impossible," whispered John to himself.

"Surely by now, you have seen enough to know that many things you thought impossible are very possible indeed."

John nodded.

"This ability allows the practitioner to affect various points on the body as well as certain organs, causing death instantly or over a period of days."

"So basically don't get touched." said John.

"If you were to face this practitioner that would be the wisest course of action." said Fujita

"Fujita Sensei, why are you telling me all this, If it's not supposed to be known?" said John.

"That, we will discuss tomorrow. It is getting late and I must rest." As if on cue, Masami appeared and stood by Fujita Sensei as he rose from the cushion.

"You will stay here tonight Kane-san. We will finish our discussion in the morning. Masami will show you to your room, please wait here." said Fujita.

John rose and bowed to the old man as he left the room. He sat down and remained seated on the cushion until Masami returned.

"Please follow me," she said in a quiet voice.

37

John stood and was about to speak when she stood still. John almost bumped into her. Masami looked around and for a moment John thought she was losing it.

"Someone is here." John didn't follow.

"What do you mean, someone is here?" said John.

Masami turned to face John, her face serene, her eyes deadly.

"Do not lose your zanshin Kane-san. Someone has come to this place to harm Fujita Sensei or you, most likely both," she said this matter of factly as she made her way to a panel in the room.

Placing her hand on it, caused it to slide back to reveal a number pad. Masami punched in a code and a section of the wall recessed and moved to the side revealing a hidden room.

"This is for Fujita Sensei, he will insist on fighting. You must not let him. Once he is inside, you and I will greet our guests." said Masami.

Fujita Sensei appeared behind them, silent as a cat.

"I will not be hiding, like some frail old man, Masami."

Masami jumped, startled by his presence.

"Fujita Sensei!" she exhaled.

"I'm old and ill but I will not be hiding in there." he pointed as he spoke.

Masami looked at John, pleading with her eyes.

"Fujita Sensei –" started John as the old man cut him off.

"Don't even begin; I was dispatching men to hell before you were off your mother's breast." said Fujita.

John opened his mouth in surprise, shut it again and then smiled, defeated.

"Ok I give up. Can we see who is trying to enter?" said John

Masami nodded and stepped over to a computer display console. Above it was a bank of monitors laid out in a grid- three by three. Each of the monitors showed a view of the exterior property in addition to sections of the interior. John could see a two man team at the door, two more figures on the roof and one person by the back door.

"Looks like five people, kind of small for an insertion team." said John

Fujita Sensei looked at the monitor.

"That is not an insertion team." said Fujita.

"How do you know?" said John.

"Because their purpose is clear." said Fujita as he stepped back.

"You mean besides breaking in."

Fujita Sensei turned and looked at John.

"Yes John, besides gaining entry, their purpose is to kill me.

The two at the front door will be the last to enter. The two above us pose the immediate threat." Fujita Sensei said to John.

"What about the rear, can't we just take out the one in the back and leave that way?"

Masami shook her head as John looked at her.

"It is a trap, even though he appears to be alone, he isn't." said Masami.

"So what's the plan? We wait them out?" said John.

"No they will not patiently wait. Their methods will grow more violent to gain entry. We are going to give them what they want, access. Masami, please open the access points." said Fujita.

Masami nodded. John was speechless for a second, then quickly recovered.

"What? You mean let them in?" said John.

"Yes, it's the one thing they wouldn't expect. In any case, this is not the real threat Kane-san." said Fujita

Masami punched in a code at the keyboard opening the front, rear and roof doors. Fujita Sensei made his way to the large living room as the assassins entered silently. Each of the five came into the living room. Two from the front entrance, two descending the stairs and one from the rear of the property. When they saw Fujita Sensei, they each drew short swords about two feet in length. Each of the swords was jet black and glistened.

"Shadow blades," whispered Masami.

Each of the five bowed briefly. Fujita Sensei nodded his head slightly. The assassins were singular in their focus-Fujita was their target. John and Masami moved to the fringe of the living room. Fujita turned in a slow circle.

"Please, whenever you are ready," he beckoned to them.

The next thirty seconds were frozen in time for John. He saw the two from the front begin to advance and in a split second, Fujita Sensei was between them. Their surprised expressions told John that they didn't expect the old man to move so fast. John couldn't see what harm Fujita Sensei could inflict; they each wore black jumpsuits that seemed to contain some kind of body armor.

They were trained and recovered from their surprise the next moment. Both sliced at Fujita Sensei, who ducked beneath the blades. He immediately rose, driving a spear hand into the throat of the one on the left. As the assassin crumpled to the floor dead, the one on the right lunged for the old man who was no longer there but behind the assassin. Using a knife hand, he snapped the neck of the assassin from behind.

The other three who were now on the opposite side of the living room drew small throwing knives. John grabbed Masami and overturned one of the futons for cover. They crouched behind it as the knives sliced through the air. John turned to see each of the knives hit their target and bounce off, falling to the floor.

Fujita Sensei picked up a few of the knives close to his feet. As the three closed the distance, Fujita Sensei threw the knives hitting two of the assassins in the neck and dropping them. The last assassin closed and began executing a downward slice with his short sword. Fujita Sensei sidestepped the slice and using a single point fist, struck the assassin three times, in three distinct areas.

Fujita Sensei stepped back and watched the last assassin fall to the ground; arms still extended overhead, blood flowing from his mouth. John stood up slowly and took in the scene. In half a minute, Fujita Sensei had killed five trained men.

John held a new respect and awe for him. Fujita Sensei turned to face John and Masami. He took a step forward and collapsed. Masami rushed to his side, with John beside her.

"John, please close the doors." said Masami. The urgency in her voice was clear as she told him the code to enter. As he made his way to the keyboard, he heard the screech of a vehicle braking outside.

"Hurry, there will be more." John punched in the code and all the doors slammed shut.

Chapter Eight
John looked around. The living room was mostly intact with the exception of the overturned futon, and the five dead bodies.

"John, the safe room quickly! We don't have much time." said Masami.

John made a motion to pick up Fujita Sensei.

"No, Kane-san, please stop." whispered Fujita.

John felt compelled to obey. Fujita's words were a rasp with steel.

"Sensei, we must get you to safety." said Masami.

"Masami that time has passed. You must keep him safe now." Fujita nodded in John's direction. Masami tried to fight back tears and failed.

"Fujita Sensei, I'm sure we can get you some help –" started John. Fujita held up his hand to stop John.

"You must leave, now. My time is complete. Even with Masami's skill, I am past that now. More will come and you must not be here when they arrive. Go to the safe room, inside you will find my journal. I hope it can be of use to you. I regret we did not get to know each other more." said Fujita.

"Sensei –" Masami whispered.

"Go. Now. Before it is too late." Fujita said as he stood.

Masami stood transfixed at this display of inner fortitude.

"Make haste Masami. Now!" Fujita yelled.

Masami, galvanized by Fujita's words, snapped into motion. She stood and grabbed John's hand, moving quickly to the safe room.

"I could try and force him –" said John.

Masami shook her head.

"You could try but you would fail. He is old, not powerless. He has chosen this to give us an opportunity; we will not waste his last gift." she said.

She punched in a code once they were in the safe room. The door that slid into place was easily two feet thick by John's guess. No one was getting in without that code. The room was comfortably furnished and roughly the size of the living room. It had everything a person needed to deal with a crisis. There was a small room off in the corner that was a bathroom. On the adjacent wall was a small kitchen with stove and sink. The opposite wall was lined with shelves holding canned goods and gallons of water.

Beside the entrance was a small desk, which looked out of place with the rest of the room. It was a deep rich mahogany and was bare of any personal effects except for a slim book sitting in the center.

"Please take the journal. I'll get the bags and change." said Masami. She made her way into one of the other small rooms in the back.

John made his way over to the desk. The journal was an old leather bound book tied in the center. John saw it was worn with age, the pages yellowed with use. Above the desk was a large monitor which flared to life as John neared the desk to pick up the journal. It showed a grid view of the interior and exterior of the property from several different angles. John touched the square that showed the living room. The square expanded to cover the whole screen. John noticed the icon in the corner, a small speaker and pressed it, engaging the audio function. Inside the safe room, John heard a muffled thump as he saw the front door come crashing in. John imagined the sound was deafening in the living room. Fujita stood unaffected by the explosion.

The sound that came over the speakers was muted. The angle of the camera took in the entire living room. John could see figures entering the room through the haze of smoke. The camera resolution allowed John to make out faces, one in particular stood out. He seemed to be the leader of the group, judging from the way he stood.

They paid no attention to the bodies on the floor. John counted three of them and heard the sharp intake of breath beside him. Masami stood beside him in a black one piece tactical suit. It was form fitting and had pockets spaced evenly on the arms and legs. A holster was attached to her right leg and short blade about two feet long was attached to the left. Her face was grim as she looked at the screen. She was looking at the leader of the group.

"Hello Sensei." The voice came over clearly through the speakers. It was the center figure who was speaking, the other two could have been statues for all the motion they exhibited. The speaker was the one that stood out. There was something about him, he looked familiar but John couldn't place him.

"I see not much has changed." Fujita sounded tired.

"Who is that?" John whispered to Masami, pointing at the speaker.

"That," she said with venom, "is what evil looks like. We must go Kane-san."

"But Fujita –" said John.

"Fujita Sensei is finished." she said. The finality in her voice surprised John.

She placed her hand on a wall to reveal a staircase that led to a tunnel. John didn't move.

"The one you see there," she said pointing at the figure in the center. "He is known as Kage – the shadow. He leads the Shadow Blades. If he is here, this is very bad."

John looked at the screen again. He looked so familiar.

"I know him from somewhere, he looks so familiar." said John. Masami looked at John and was about to speak when a voice came over the speakers.

"It is time to end things Sensei." Kage said

For the first time Kage looked around as if seeing the bodies for the first time. "I see you still have some skill, but you are looking tired, Sensei."

"That title is no longer yours to use," said Fujita.

Two more figures entered and stood by the entrance to the living room.

Kage bowed. "I understand."

In a split second he produced a katana, a three foot razor sharp sword with a slightly curved blade. It happened so fast John barely registered the movement. If it wasn't for his ability to blur he would have missed it completely. One moment Kage was across the room, the next he was beside Fujita Sensei. The sword protruded through Fujita's body. As he withdrew the blade, Fujita began to fall. Kage caught him, a look of sadness that was quickly masked, crossed his face. He laid the body on the floor and motioned to the men who came in with him.

"Take the body. He will be honored as his position deserves." said Kage.

When all four men left the room, Kage turned, his eyes wet. "Goodbye grandfather." he said.

As they headed for the stairs, John grabbed Masami's arm.

"That is one seriously screwed up family!" said John.

"If he did not do this, he would have been killed. He had no choice." said Masami.

"There is always a choice!" said John.

"No, John there is always the illusion of choice." said Masami.

She headed down the stairs.

Chapter Nine

Mikaela was livid. This was an uncommon state for her. She was always in control of her emotions. She stood beside one of her best computer operatives.

"What do you mean, there is no trace?" she said in a measured voice.

Her words became clipped when she was upset, and she had passed upset ten minutes ago. The computer operator kept typing as if he didn't hear her. Mikaela drew a long breath and exhaled slowly.

"Robert, explain to me how that is possible." she said.

Robert shrugged. He was the best hacker employed by the CATT – the Cyber Anti-Terrorism Taskforce. He had no fear for the ice queen, as Mikaela was known, because he worked directly for David Soros, the Director of CATT. This didn't mean he aggravated her when she was clearly angry. He was oblivious, not suicidal.

"Ms. Petrovich, this unit has no evidence of anyone using it for anything outside of normal routine activities. If you were alerted and someone was on this terminal, they are good."

"Better than you?" she goaded.

"If they can vanish like this –" he said as he pointed at the monitor, "Then they can be part of TU – The Unknown." said Robert.

"Really." Mikaela said as she gave it some thought. "That means he or she is at an elite level which narrows it down considerably. Names, Robert, I need names, yesterday."

"Guaranteed to be a short list," said Robert as he typed at his terminal.

"If this person is good enough to be part of The Unknown, it better be. You have one hour before I'm back for it. Make sure the information is relevant. You know where I'll be." she said.

It was indicative of her position that Mikaela had unrestricted access to the Director of CATT. She never needed an appointment or a call. She simply went to his office on the lowest level in the facility, which descended ten stories underground.

Despite being nearly one hundred feet underground, the lowest level gave the impression of space. The director's level was a U-shaped affair, with glass panels separating it from a garden in the center. The garden itself was an area which always pleasantly surprised her. A small pond contained exotic fish. A small foot bridge allowed access to a Zen rock garden in the center. Running water could be heard but Mikaela never found its source.

What appeared to be glass was actually two inch thick lexan, rated to stop most small projectiles. The lexan itself was electronically charged, so that by running a current through it, it became opaque, enshrouding the garden in a simulated fog. The director's main area was situated in the center of the U.

It was rumored David never left the facility. The level was spacious enough for living quarters, and Mikaela had never seen the Director outside of this level, much less the facility. As she crossed the garden, she took note of the cleverly hidden counter measures strategically placed around the space. Infrared sensors camouflaged as flowers. Floor panel triggers disguised to look like flat stones and an assortment of others. She smiled to herself as she realized that those were the ones she could see. She could only imagine the ones that were hidden even to her. The garden, which looked tranquil and beautiful, was a deathtrap to the uninitiated. One wrong step could literally be your last. The garden always made you tread carefully.

Very much like Mikaela herself.

"Mika, I'm in the observatory, please visit." a voice floated down to her.

Only one person could call her that and walk away unscathed.

Mikaela made her way through the office space until she came to the left side of the U. On the far wall were thirty monitors each displaying different areas of the facility on a rotating loop.

Opposite that wall was one monitor which encompassed the entire wall. Seated before the large monitor was a man in his mid-fifties, his black hair cut short was starting to show some grey at the temples. He dressed casually in black slacks and a crisp white shirt. The shirt offset the blue-green in his eyes. Taller than average, she could tell he was still training. He looked like he would be more at home in the mountains somewhere than an office. Mikaela took a long appraising look at him, and then sat in one of the chairs, situated to face the large monitor wall.

"Hello David." she said.

"It's nice of you to visit, Mika. I hear you came up dry on that computer you appropriated." said David.

It was uncanny how quickly he knew things; she figured he couldn't run a group like CATT without that expertise though.

"I'm trying another angle. I think it will pan out." said Mikaela.

David looked at her a moment and then tapped a few keys on his modified wrist keyboard. An image appeared on the large monitor.

"Do you know who this is?" David said, as he turned to face the image.

"No, should I?" asked Mikaela.

"Mikaela, this man is going to make your life very complicated." said David.

Mikaela hated complicated. She sighed. "Who is he and why do I care?"

David handed her a thick folder.

"We have a situation with one of our assets and he was on site." said David.

Situation was David's code for clusterfuck, so Mikaela knew this was serious.

"Which asset?" said Mikaela.

"Takashi 'Jiro' Fujita is presumed missing or dead-he missed his last call in and he has never missed a call in, ever. I think this man was involved in some way." said David.

"How do we know he was on site?" said Mikaela.

"Surveillance picked him up on the property near the time in question. Is it possible he knew about the asset?" said David as he turned to her .

"Not possible. Fujita was in a secure location known to us only, aside from that he may have been old, but he was highly skilled. In addition, Masami Murakami is his assistant/nurse and she is nothing to sneeze at. Even I would think twice before tangling with her." she said.

"And yet despite all of that, this person was seen entering a level one secure location and more importantly, not exiting. You need to find him. I want to have a conversation with him."

"I'm guessing that means alive." she said.

"Well, since I haven't learned to commune with the dead, I would prefer breathing, yes." said David.

"Is he going to survive the conversation?" asked Mikaela.

"That depends on what he has to say." said David.

Mikaela turned to view the image that was on the screen looking at her.

It was an image of John Kane.

Chapter Ten

She knew they would be after her. She counted on it in fact. Her sensei had prepared her for the eventuality, taught her how to blend and be invisible. So far she had been able to remain undetected. She knew it couldn't last, sooner or later, they would discover who she was. Part of her knew this was a suicide mission. She was prepared for that too.

Killing assets was dangerous task, despite her training; she ran a real risk every time she eliminated one. It was always possible they were better trained or that the asset in question was part of a trap to eliminate her. She had been careful, covering her tracks, changing identities often, staying off the grid as much as possible. They tricky part was avoiding the cameras. They were everywhere. She was grateful she didn't live in London. The CCTV net would have discovered her in short order. Being in New York City was no cake walk. Cameras were everywhere but she took measures to avoid them as best she could.

Today she was training in one of the older martial arts schools in Brooklyn. It was almost impossible to find without her sensei's help since it was a non-descript warehouse housing the school. The Sensei who ran the school was a throwback to a different era that believed progress was measured in sweat, tears and blood. It was the training she was used to. It was the type of training that had forged her character and spirit, making her the weapon she was today.

They were sparring today. The Sensei, recognizing her level of skill, allowed her to train with the seniors.

She made a conscious effort to fight without any hidden ability, at first this was difficult, she was used to being her abilities that disconnecting from them made it almost impossible. With practice, she became better at it. Today as she stood facing a tall senior, who rippled with muscle under his uniform, she realized that her ability gave her an unfair advantage and made a mental note to fight fair, mostly. She had to remember not to attract too much attention to herself.

She looked around and noticed she was the only female on the line. She wasn't the only female in the school but she was the only one on the floor the Sensei allowed to fight the men. The senior she stood in front of didn't know her. He took one look at her diminutive size and made an assessment. She had seen it happen hundreds of times before.

Her Sensei's words came back to her. *When an opponent sees you and dismisses you because of your appearance. Use it. Feign weakness but respond with strength.* That is exactly what her opponent had done. One of the reasons she trained here was that the Sensei didn't believe in any type of fighting gear. Punches to the head were encouraged as well as groundwork and grappling. In essence, among the seniors, almost anything was allowed. She liked that, a lot.

I hope Sensei lets me stay here longer than the last school.

The Sensei signaled them to begin and the four pairs faced each other, bowed and began to circle.

He towered over her. She barely cleared five feet and he was easily over six. In a moment, she saw several openings and decided she would wait until he made a move. He opened with a front snap kick. She side stepped it, noticing the power and realizing he intended to hit her, good. At least he wasn't one of those who saw her and toned it down because she was female and small.

She began to circle around, aware of the distance she needed to execute her techniques. He circled with her. He closed the distance in an instant, unleashing several punches at her head. She evaded most of them, he was slow. She let the last one glance off her right cheek. It had the desired effect.

He was arrogant and it surfaced. She smiled, this fight was over. He just didn't know it yet. He jabbed twice with the left, setting her up for the right cross she knew was coming. As his right hand came at her, she slipped to her outside left. For a second the surprise registered on his face. For her, a second was a lifetime. She dipped slightly and drove a right elbow into his solar plexus.

The body is an amazing machine. With sufficient impact to the nerve cluster that makes up the solar plexus, the body has a cascading reaction. Chief among them is the expulsion of air, followed closely by a loss of strength to the legs.

As he forcefully exhaled, she reached up and grabbed his right arm. Bending it at the elbow towards his ear, she unleashed a joint kick at the back of his right knee. This was only sparring, so she didn't shatter it. The kick allowed her to use leverage. As he fell backwards, she straightened his arm, locking it at the elbow and took it just shy of dislocating the shoulder. He was face down on the floor and gasping for breath. It had happened so fast, he was still reeling from the elbow strike. He quickly tapped the floor as she started to pull the arm towards herself threatening dislocation.

She stepped back and let him stand up. The Sensei signaled all to stop. One of the other seniors walked over to her opponent and asked if he could continue. He nodded; she felt his anger coming off in waves. The senior was red faced from embarrassment and anger as he stood to face her again.

He would be dangerous now that his ego was bruised. It was a matter of saving face now. She wondered why she did this, but she knew: It was the closest thing to death she could get, that and this is where she thrived. She needed the edge.

He was angry but now he would be reckless. They stood facing each other again and bowed. The Sensei signaled for them to begin. It was just them on the floor now. She allowed her awareness to expand and took in the dojo. *Always keep your zanshin in place.* She could hear her sensei's voice in her head. Everything was connected. She took it all in, the other students, the space itself. She observed it all and then let it go. In an instant, it was only her and her opponent. This was right, this was pure. She took a deep breath, silently thanked her sensei for placing her on this path and met the oncoming attack.

Chapter Eleven

The tunnel was dimly lit as Masami made her way down the stairs.

"Where does this tunnel head?" asked John.

"This tunnel leads to a garage where we will have access to a vehicle." said Masami.

"Sounds like a great idea. Put some distance between us and them." said John.

Masami didn't answer.

Then it hit John, slowly at first, a nagging thought, then stronger.

"Masami, wait a second, if they knew about this place, the building I mean, wouldn't they know about the garage?"

"It is unlikely but not impossible. We need to be careful." she said slowly.

They had reached the end of the tunnel. John figured they were about two blocks from the property. Before he opened the door, Masami touched his arm. John turned to face her.

"Back there, why didn't you use your ability? Fujita Sensei told me you are skilled." said Masami.

"I made a promise long ago, that I would never use it again." said John.

Masami remained silent for a moment.

"It is my belief that you will not be able to honor this promise for very much longer." she said.

John was thinking the same thing as he opened the door. The door opened to a large converted storage space that housed about five vehicles of different makes and models. All of them were luxury vehicles. John had that tickling feeling again. It was an instinct he had learned to listen to early on in his life.

"Masami, this is too easy. I don't like it." he said as he looked at the vehicles.

"What do you mean too easy? I told you it was unlikely that anyone-" said Masami.

John felt the explosion before actually hearing it. The wave of compressed air buffeted him and triggered his response as reflex. As it always happened when he blurred, time crawled to a standstill. Grabbing Masami, he pushed her back into the corridor pulling the door behind him, when the whump of pressure hit. He was certain ribs and possibly more was broken.

They fell into the corridor as a wave of fire rolled towards them. Masami, who had been shielded from the pressure wave by John's body, had the presence of mind to close the door as one of the vehicles or what remained of it slammed into it. John crumpled to the floor, his breath ragged.

"Good thing it was unlikely." Those were the last words he said before passing out.

Back at the property the man called Kage looked into the night and noticed the explosion. It would be hard to miss given the magnitude of it.

"It seems Fujita Sensei was not alone. Go and see if anyone survived that." He pointed at the explosion. "If they did, which I doubt, make sure they aren't breathing by the time you leave the area. Go now." Two men took off on motorcycles rushing to the site of the explosion.

What were you doing, old man? Kage thought as he entered his vehicle.

"Follow them, but avoid the police. We don't need this getting any more attention than it already has." said Kage to his driver.

The driver sped off in the direction of the explosion.

Chapter Twelve

How do you find someone who doesn't want to be found? You go to his last known location and start looking there. Mikaela was driving to the Queens property when she noticed the fire trucks and ambulances racing past her.

"Follow them, Gustav." she said.

He knew her long enough to go with her instincts. He switched lanes and kept pace with the emergency vehicles. Something told her this was right. She had achieved everything she had because she learned to listen to her intuition. Right now that intuition was telling her that this was relevant.

"Gus, approach it from the other side. Let's keep it low profile." Gustav nodded.

Mikaela looked at the folder Robert had prepared for her. It was thin with too little information. The list with known whereabouts was five names long. She rubbed the bridge of her nose to stave off the impending headache. She dialed Robert.

"This list you gave me is thin." Her words were clipped short.

"That is the short list." *Robert or better yet David wouldn't keep relevant information from her, would he?*

"Well the first three I know couldn't pull this off, at least not when they ran with me. I doubt they have improved that much." said Mikaela.

"And the last two?" said Robert.

"One is on loan to Interpol. He may have the skill but not the motivation," said Mikaela.

"That leaves Cheung." Robert paused. "It says here deceased. You think the dead guy did this?" asked Robert.

Mikaela gave it some thought. When you eliminate every possibility, what remained was truth.

"We're here," said Gustav beside her. She snapped out of reverie.

"Yes Robert, track down the dead guy. I want to know when he died and how. I want to see a grave. I want a body. Something smells here." said Mikaela.

"This is going to take a while, Ms. Petrovich."

"Robert —"her voice made her message clear.

"Got it, top shelf it. I will call you with the info." said Robert.

"Thank you," she said and hung up.

She opened the door as Gustav parked and headed to the explosion.

"Let's see what we can see," she said to herself.

Chapter Thirteen

John ached all over. Somewhere far away someone was calling him. It had been years since he had blurred and his body was reminding him. That voice, somehow it sounded familiar. His thoughts were a jumbled mess.

"John!"

There it was again, someone calling him; somehow he felt he should recognize the voice. Part of his brain was yelling at him to get up and move, the other part was all in favor of a nice nap. It was the excruciating pain that brought him back and stole his breath as he gasped seeing stars.

"What the –" then it all rushed back. "Masami, you OK?"

"Yes, thanks to you. Now let me help you. I had to press on this to bring you back. It looked as if you were going to remain unconscious and I cannot carry you." she said.

She began to manipulate the bones in his right forearm. John clenched his teeth against the pain.

"Is that really necessary? I'm conscious now." John said through the haze of pain.

"It is if you want to use your arm in the near future." said Masami.

She placed both hands on his arm, for a second John almost pulled away reflexively. Her hands were hot, no not hot, burning. He looked down, half expecting to see burning flesh. Masami's hands were a dull red, the way your hand looked when you shone a flashlight through it. The internal glow stopped at her wrist. She removed her hands and lifted John's right arm. It felt like someone had shoved a hot poker into his sides.

"Ribs are broken, this is going to hurt." said Masami.

"You mean hurt more, right?" John said through clenched teeth.

She nodded and placed a hand on his ribs, knitting bone and tissue. John nearly screamed in agony. He bit his lip until he tasted blood, willing himself not to cry out. Masami focused on his side a little longer then removed her hand.

"I apologize for doing this so abruptly but I don't think time is a luxury we have." she said.

John nodded, his voice gone for a moment.

"We must go back to the house. They will not expect that, also it is our only means of exit since this way is blocked."

They both looked at the door that had been pushed in by the force of a vehicle and the blast. There was no way that door was opening from the inside without the use of power tools.

"Thank you," said Masami bowing. "If you had kept your vow, we would most likely be dead."

"Seems my body is smarter than my brain." said John.

"Your body reacted to the immediate danger. This is the result of many years of training." said Masami.

John thought about that for a second. What had triggered the blur? He couldn't pinpoint the exact moment, but he was glad his body had more sense than his brain.

John returned the bow.

"Thank you, I feel almost brand new." he said.

He flexed his right arm, testing the forearm, and then he raised his arm. The pain wasn't entirely gone but it had been reduced to a dull throb, instead of a bright sun of agony.

"Let's go," he said.

Someone had rigged the cars to explode and did an excellent job of it. The converted space was an inferno.

Someone knew about the garage. John didn't know who that was, but he was going to find out.

Chapter Fourteen

Mikaela and Gustav headed over to the garage, or what was left of it.

"Gustav, talk to me." said Mikaela.

Gustav looked around with a dispassionate eye. He stepped around the vehicles that were mostly intact burned out husks. He bent down and inspected the undercarriages noticing the origin points of the explosions.

"It looks like they were all rigged to blow." said Gustav.

"All of them, why?" she said.

"Covering the angles, making sure no one walked away from this." He said that last part as he outstretched his hand, pointing to the wrecks.

"Do you see any bodies?" she said.

Mikaela was looking at the wreckage. Gustav went to each of the vehicles then came back to where she was standing. He shook his head, no bodies.

"So what does that tell us?" she said.

Gustav remained silent for a moment. He enjoyed these tests she gave him; it made him feel useful and important.

"It could have been several things. They could've gotten spooked and headed back, there are two exits. Or the detonation went off early barbecuing them and we have some very well done critters on the other side of that door." he said as he pointed to the smashed door that had saved the lives of John and Masami.

"Let's find out which it is, before I die of excitement." said Mikaela.

The emergency service personnel were filling the garage, along with the police and fire department vehicles.

"Hey! Who are you? You can't be here!" An officer approached Mikaela.

"DHS, we think this explosion may be linked to a terrorist cell operating in this area." said Mikaela.

She showed her credentials which were authentic. CATT, which didn't officially exist, operated under the Department of Homeland Security umbrella as one of the fringe organizations. In the case of CATT, it was on the outer fringe.

"Sorry ma'am," said the officer not totally convinced. "I'm going to have to clear this with my supervisor, please wait here."

"I understand, Officer – O'Reilly, is it? By all means, clear it with your supervisor." said Mikaela.

The police officer went into the crowd to find his supervisor, checking back periodically on the pair.

Mikaela gestured at the door and Gustav moved. Grabbing a crow bar from the trunk of one of the vehicles, he stepped around the car that had blocked the doorway. The door, which was mangled, came off its hinges after some coaxing with the crow bar. Gustav pulled the door away and looked into the corridor.

"All clear." said Gustav.

"Let's see where this leads." said Mikaela.

She walked past Gustav. Gustav reached into his shoulder holster and pulled out his Glock as he followed her down the corridor. This whole setup smelled wrong to him, he thought as he kept pace with Mikaela.

No one noticed the two EMS first responders who were searching among the wreckage. They blended in with the multitude. Once satisfied there were no bodies to be recovered, they made their way out of the garage.

The bodies of the actual EMS responders would be discovered much later. One of them pulled out a cell phone and made a call.

Kage had no patience for failure.

"No bodies have been discovered sir."

Kage thought about this a moment.

"Very well, before you head back, go to the property and sanitize it. Call in a team if you have to. I will see you at the compound."

"Yes sir."

He hung up the phone and turned to his partner.

"We go back and sanitize." The second man nodded, started his motorcycle and headed back to the property, followed by the first.

Chapter Fifteen

Time is elastic. Most people didn't understand this, but she knew it to be true.

"Begin!" the Sensei's voice boomed across the dojo floor. The senior standing across from her bowed. As she bowed in return, he unleashed an axe kick designed to land on the top of her head. Sensing this she focused her breath and felt time slow. Blurring slightly allowed her to avoid the kick. The leg crashed down onto the hardwood floor, where she stood moments earlier.

She became smoke, an illusion. Everything he threw at her missed by a fraction of an inch. She kept it close because she didn't need the unwanted attention. She didn't notice the eyes of one of the women following the fight. Each time she blurred, the woman watching knew exactly where to look.

The senior fighting her was angry and getting frustrated, making his techniques sloppy. It was time to end this.

Her first strikes were light, just taps to let him know that she could touch him. He smiled as she hit him, thinking this was the extent of her strength. He unleashed a two punch and kick combination, confident in his power. It was time to show him what power felt like. She slipped past the two punches, evading them easily. His kick was a front snap kick that would have shattered any part of her, had it hit. At the last possible second, she blurred inside the kick avoiding the leg and struck his inner thigh several times. It took a moment for the pain to register. She stepped back as he looked at her in confusion. Once the leg touched the floor, the searing pain exploded, rendering the leg useless. The senior crumpled to the floor, grabbing his leg.

"She's got a knife or some kind of weapon!" he yelled.

"Stop!" yelled the Sensei. "Sarah, please come here."

That was the name she gave them. As she stepped forward the Sensei took her hands in his own and after a moment nodded.

"Show me where you hit him." said the Sensei.

She pointed to the exact locations on her leg as she was shown. The points she struck were designed to be hit in sequence to disrupt; a different sequence would have had a fatal outcome.

The Sensei nodded again," You will stay after class, we must talk."

It was the last thing she wanted, yet she found herself bowing saying "Hai- yes Sensei."

Chapter Sixteen

John and Masami arrived at the house. They entered the safe room and looked out into the living room through the monitors. John didn't like the idea of coming back, every instinct told him to get as far away from there as possible. As they left the safe room, Masami punched in a code that would prevent the door from being opened from the inside.

The bodies of the Shadow Blades lay where they had fallen.

"We must leave quickly, they will be back to erase their presence." said Masami.

Masami pointed at the bodies. John couldn't agree more. What had been a feeling of unease was now a klaxon going off in his head.

"The sooner the better." said John.

The short sword aimed for his heart only missed because of John's training. At the last moment John flinched, some part of his brain registering the danger and the blade sliced across his left bicep, drawing blood moments later. A figure stepped out of the shadows, facing John. A second figure came downstairs, took in the scene and drew a gun.

"I'm guessing they're already here," John said.

Two Shadow blades dressed in EMS uniforms faced him. They were fast, just not fast enough. John shifted his weight and blurred; his body screaming at him from several different directions. He had forgotten how much he enjoyed it, the sensation of speed, and calm occurring simultaneously.

He stopped behind the Shadow Blade that had cut him. He could smell the leather of his jacket, the gel in his hair, even his deodorant. Every time he blurred, his senses were kicked into overdrive. Too late the Shadow Blade began to turn. John grabbed his head and twisted sharply to the side. He felt the neck give, twist and snap like dry twigs in the winter. The second Shadow Blade had raised his gun and was pulling the trigger. His arm flew up in a graceful arc landing several feet away, shots going wide. Masami had crossed the distance and removed the Shadow Blades arm in one smooth motion.

John fell to one knee, spent. His body was in no shape for this much use. The second Blade ran for the door as Masami made her way to John. John's left arm started throbbing and his shirt sleeve was soaked with blood. He tried standing and the floor shifted into a tilt that made him think better of it.

"I need a moment," he said, voice ragged.

He was winded and tired. The blurring was catching up to him.

"I'm afraid a moment is all we can spare, he will bring others." said Masami.

"He should be dead within the hour, you sliced off his arm."

"Kage and his Blades possess a form of my skill, a corruption that allows them to work with poison. He will not die from this wound." said Masami.

"Then let's get out of here." John was able to walk without the room spinning and started heading to the door. Masami grabbed his arm.

"Not that way. Up." she said.

Masami pointed to the stairs.

"This will be faster," said John.

"The roof will allow us access to the adjacent building. It will be safer." said Masami.

John stopped, in his rush to get out of the property, he had stopped thinking operationally. The roof would be the hardest of the three exists to guard. Which meant it was the best choice as their exit.

"Let me see your arm, maybe I can stop some of the bleeding." said Masami. "You were fortunate the blade was not poisoned."

Masami put her hand on his arm and staunched the flow of blood. He could see the tissue knitting itself.

Sweat broke out on her forehead but that was the only indication that what she was doing was an exertion for her.

"You're much better at this than I am." said John.

"I have not interrupted my training as you have. Therefore the cost is significantly less." said Masami.

They headed upstairs to the roof.

"I would appreciate if you both stopped where you are and turned around slowly. Any sudden moves and I shoot the one I do see. Are we clear?" said a voice behind them.

Mikaela stood facing the stairs, her gun drawn, while Gustav covered the stairs from the living room. There was no way John could get to both of them even if he wasn't hurt. He turned slowly with his hands in the air. Masami did the same.

Chapter Seventeen

The Sensei closed the class with the traditional bowing. As the seniors faced the Sensei and bowed, Sarah saw the senior she had fought looking at her. He was definitely not a fan. She didn't give it much thought; more than anything it was his ego that was bruised. She bowed like everyone else then sat off in a corner on her knees, in the kneeling position called seiza, and waited for the Sensei. He spoke to a few students about their techniques during the class, asked after the families of a few others and wished them a good evening. He locked the door then walked over to the dojo floor. He sat in the center of the floor, took a deep breath and looked at the young woman who called herself Sarah. Without looking in her direction, he spoke.

"What is your name?" he said.

His voice much quieter now still held a core of steel.

"Sarah, Sensei," she said.

He waved his hand as if swatting a mosquito.

"This is not your name. What is your true name?" he said.

She remained motionless for a full twenty seconds.

"I cannot say, Sensei." she said.

The Sensei turned to face her.

"Now that is the truth. Come and face me, Sarah who is not Sarah." said the Sensei.

She stood and walked over to where he sat, sitting before him about four feet away. He stood and she did the same.

"You may attack when you are ready." said the Sensei.

"Sensei?" she wasn't sure she heard him correctly.

"Was I not clear?" asked the Sensei.

"No Sensei. I mean yes Sensei, you were clear."

She had not expected this. She thought it was going to be the usual barrage of questions. Where did she train and with whom? She had never been asked to fight before. Who was this Sensei?

"You are perhaps considering if you can use all of your skill. Please feel free." said the Sensei.

The Sensei bowed and took a relaxed stance. There was no way she could use all of her ability, she could seriously hurt or injure him, and she liked this Sensei. She would only go half speed and make sure not to put him in a hospital. She stepped close, about two feet away and bowed. He bowed in return, a slight smile crossing his face.

She lunged with a spear hand aimed for his throat, pulling it slightly so she wouldn't crush his larynx, but just enough to make him gag and possibly give this whole fight idea up. Her fingertips were about to hit when he shifted ninety degrees causing her to miss.

Missed! She never missed, or miscalculated. *What the hell was going on?*

There he stood, just an inch away from her fingers. *Was it possible he read her strike?* He could just be very skilled and picked up on some minute tell and just shifted out of the way.

It was possible but improbable. She attacked again, a driving knife hand to the collar bone, followed by an uppercut to the chin. He countered with a wrist block to push the knife hand out of range, while tucking his chin, letting her uppercut sail past his face.

He turned 180 degrees outside her knife hand and tapped her in the back of the head. He took a few steps back and waited. She turned to face him. He was fast and he had skill. She took a deep breath. *Fine, you want full speed you get it.* She focused her will and blurred, driving a fist to his solar plexus. She didn't want to hurt him, just wind him, so he could realize he bit off more than he could chew. As she closed the distance, he stepped inside her strike, grabbed her arm while turning his back to her. He bent over and threw her across the dojo floor where she landed ungraciously on her ass.

"What the–how did you?" she said as she slowly stood.

"That was quite fast, Sarah. Just not fast enough," he said as bowed.

She stood there for a moment in a daze. No one outside her Sensei had been able to see her, much less counter while she blurred. *Who was this Sensei?*

"You need to hone your skill, if you wish to surpass your current level. Is this something you wish?" asked the Sensei.

She nodded. "Yes, yes it is."

"Good then we will start with the basics. Tomorrow, but first, we will start with introductions. I am Himara Sensei. My full name is Sato Fujita Himara."

His eyes burned into hers, his face unreadable.

"And what is your name?"

She paused for a moment, knowing that he would sense if she lied. She needed his help. Could she risk it? She would have to.

"My name is Kei, Kei Kanegisha."

Chapter Eighteen

"How did you exit the safe room?" asked Masami.

"I was quite the hacker in a previous life, Mrs. Murakami, yes?" said Mikaela.

Masami nodded slightly.

"Not that it was easy. I've just had a lot of practice."

"I will keep that in mind for the future. Mrs.?"

"Petrovich, Mikaela Petrovich."

"Thank you. Now how can we help you?" said Masami.

John looked at Masami incredulously. Masami was nonplussed.

"I have to take you both into custody for the assassination and-or kidnapping of one Takashi Jiro Fujita," said Mikaela.

"It appears you have been misinformed Mrs. Petrovich. We had nothing to do with Fujita Sensei's demise."

Something nagged at Mikaela, something she couldn't quite pin down.

"How is it that you came to be here, Mr. Kane?" said Mikaela.

"Listen, we don't have time!" said John.

"No, you listen! I'm asking questions and expect answers. So I'm going to ask again. How is it that you are on this property, Mr. Kane?" said Mikaela.

John opened his mouth to answer when three grenades sailed into the hallway, coming to rest at the foot of the stairs. Gustav grabbed Mikaela, his training taking over and shielded her with his body. John and Masami ran upstairs as the world turned white and filled with flame.

The ground floor was an inferno. The lower half of the stairs was gone. John headed down anyway.

"What are you doing?" said Masami.

"I have to be sure," John said as he jumped down the remaining three steps. The entire staircase seemed unstable now. John made his way to the living room and found Gustav lying over Mikaela. John rolled Gustav's body to check his neck for a pulse but realized it would be futile. The left side of his neck was gone. Underneath his body lay Mikaela who groaned when John moved Gustav.

John scooped her up, conscious of the fact that he might be making something worse by moving her. He knew that if he left her, she would share Gustav's fate.

"Nothing is worse than dead," he said to himself as he headed for the stairs. Masami stood ready to take Mikaela from John. Masami took her and quickly made her way up to the roof; John trailed behind her, as the stairs collapsed behind him. They crossed over to an adjoining roof when John heard a whump that he felt in his abdomen.

"What the hell was that?" asked john.

"That was a sanitizer. The Shadow Blades use it to remove any trace of their presence." said Masami. "What of her associate?"

"Dead." said John.

"If he wasn't, he is now. The sanitizer is basically several large acid bombs that disintegrate everything in their blast radius, especially flesh." said Masami.

"Nasty." said John.

"Yes it is and very efficient. No bodies to move or take care of and afterwards they send a cleaning crew to make sure there are no traces left." said Masami.

"And this is why no one believes Shadow Blades exist?" said John.

"That and they leave no witnesses, ever."

"What are we going to do with her?" asked John.

"I cannot help her much now. My body – I need some rest." said Masami.

"Hospital?" said John.

Masami shook her head slowly.

"She would be dead by morning." said Masami.

"Let me see if I can get us some help." said John.

John pulled out his cell and pressed the only number it was programmed to call.

"John! Thank God. I thought you were dead, old man." said Mole.

"Not for lack of trying. Mole we need some help."

"We? Who is we John?" said Mole.

"Three of us right now. We need to access a place off the grid and under the radar." said John.

"Anyone I know?" said Mole.

"Remember the picture I sent you, Mikaela Petrovich?"

There was pause and John thought he had lost the call.

"Mole?" said John.

"John, shit. Tell me you're kidding. Tell me you are not running around with the ice queen." said Mole.

"The what?" said John.

"The. Ice. Queen. Yes with capitals. She's bad mojo, John, very bad mojo. As in run the other way bad." said Mole.

"I was in the process of that when the grenades – never mind Mole. Look, she's hurt and we need a place to crash."

"Take her to a hospital John. Trust me; you want space between you and her, lots and lots of it. Preferably a continent if you can arrange it. Remember you asked me to get information on her? I still haven't found anything on her John. I haven't found anything, John. Not one thing on her. This is me we're talking about." said Mole.

John understood what the Mole was trying to say but he had no choice.

"Can't, some very nasty bad men want her dead." said John.

"Ok, your funeral, who is the other person?" said Mole.

"Trust me when I tell you that even you wouldn't know her." said John.

"John, you're my hero. I leave you alone for a few hours and you manage to find time to snag the ice queen and some mystery woman? You are the man." said Mole.

"Mole, the address please." said John.

"OK, got it. I'll text it to you, encrypted. Use our cipher."

"I need a car as well." said John.

"Where is the drop off?"

John told him the location.

"There is too much activity over there with some explosion and then some firebombing of a property not too far away. Wait, was that you?" asked Mole.

"No Mole," John lied knowing that the truth would set Mole on some other tangent.

71

"Good, because whoever is responsible has gotten mucho attention and I know you don't like attention. Ok, can you make it to a gas station on Northern Blvd and 36th Street, that's about four blocks from where you are."

John looked at Masami, who nodded.

"Yes, we can. What's our window?"

"Ten minutes." said Mole.

"Mole –" John was not pleased. Ten minutes would be cutting it close.

"Hey this is beyond short notice. I don't even want to think about what I will have to do just to get you these ten minutes."

"Fine, we'll make it." said John.

"Good, I'll make sure it's a Phaeton. I know you prefer them."

"Thanks Mole."

"Thank me from the car. Your ten minutes starts now."

"We have to move, fast," said John.

"So I heard." said Masami, who was running for the stairs. John picked up Mikaela, headed up after Masami, conscious of each passing second.

They made it in eight minutes thanks to Masami who knew the area well. John approached the Phaeton from the driver's side. As vehicles went, it was one of John's favorites. They were large with plenty of trunk space. There was much to be said for German engineering. As John approached, the door opened and a slim blonde woman stepped out, and opened the rear door for him.

"Hello Iris," said John. The woman gave him a curt nod and handed him a set of keys.

"Mr. Kane." said Iris.

"Standard protocol?" said John.

"Correct. Bullet proof lexan, armor plating, nitrous oxide and finger print recognition on keys and interior."

"Disposal?" said John.

"The usual, leave it parked and press the alarm button, either inside the car or on the key, and we will retrieve and sanitize."

"Thank you Iris."

She nodded again and walked to the other side of the gas station, a black Suburban pulled up and she stepped inside, the darkened glass obscured her and the driver from view as they pulled away.

John entered the vehicle. Masami was seated in the rear with Mikaela trying to comfort her and checking for any serious injury. John placed his thumb on a special panel in the dash, after three seconds a computerized voice notified him that his print was recognized and the car started. John pulled out his phone and checked his texts. The address was located somewhere in downtown Manhattan. He called Mole.

"Did you make it?" asked Mole.

"I did."

"Who did they send?"

"Iris this time." said John.

Mole whistled. "They must really respect you to send out Iris; hardly anyone gets to see her, John."

"I feel privileged."

"You should, she's leet." said Mole.

"She's what?"

"Leet, means elite, she's one of the best."

"Thank you for the English lesson. This address, are you certain?"

"The best I could do on short notice. You will be good there max one week, then I suggest relocating." said Mole.

"That's plenty of time."

"I figured. Usual SOP, don't attract attention. Don't go outside, you know the drill. Make sure your guests do too. Talk to you later." said Mole.

Mole hung up. He was never for long conversations, no matter how secure the line was.

John pulled out and headed west on Northern Blvd.

"Where are we going?" asked Masami.

"I'd rather not say." John could hear Mikaela stirring. "Some place safe."

"I don't think such a place exists Kane-san." said Masami.

John didn't answer, but deep down he agreed.

Chapter Nineteen

Kei had never trained so hard in her life. Grueling did not begin to describe it. The fight with the senior felt like ages ago. She couldn't believe it was only earlier in the day.

"You lack focus, your ability is still-" he paused, searching for the right word.

"Untapped?" she volunteered. He looked at her in a way that would have withered other students.

"I was going to say rudimentary, basic," said Himara.

That stung her. Red faced she bit her tongue and stifled her response. The door to the dojo opened and Himara Sensei paused.

"Ah, good finally, now you begin to work." said Himara.

Kei couldn't believe her ears. She had just been training for four hours and now she would begin? A thin woman stepped into the dojo. Her grey eyes took in the scene. She bowed to Himara Sensei. He returned the bow. It was the woman who watched her fight and managed to follow her every move.

"Please get dressed, so you can assist Kei with her training," said Himara.

She bowed in response and went off to change.

"Who is that, she looks familiar." said Kei.

"That is your training partner. She will help polish your skills. Steel against steel, sharpens." said Himara.

With that Himara Sensei left Kei on the dojo floor alone. The woman returned a few minutes later, dressed simply in a plain white uniform. A black belt devoid of markings or rank was tied around her waist.

"My name is Lea. It is my honor to train with you today." She bowed.

"I'm Kei, thank you for training with me. I guessed I pissed off the Sensei. He doesn't even want to train me."

Lea smiled and shook her head, letting Kei know she was wrong.

"If he did not want you trained, I would not be here. Now I know you're warmed up. Are you ready?"

Kei took a breath, got into a fighting stance and faced Lea.

"As ready as I –" Kei never finished the sentence as the air was forced out of her lungs. Lea had slammed a palm strike into Kei's chest, sending her sliding across the dojo floor.

"I'm going to guess that you were not ready," said Lea.

Kei lifted her sore body from the hardwood floor. As she stood, she smiled at Lea.

"Are you ready now?" said Lea.

The question is, are you? thought Kei, as she blurred towards her.

Chapter Twenty

John pulled into the garage across from the Essex restaurant. He double checked the address before getting out of the car. The address was the building across from the Essex. Once an industrial area, the lofts had been converted into huge apartments. It was one of these lofts that would be their base of operations for the next week. John opened the door while Masami assisted Mikaela who had regained consciousness and was walking, somewhat unsteadily.

"How long can we stay here?" said Masami as she helped Mikaela towards the door.

"A week at most, with no outside contact." said John.

Mikaela, fully conscious now turned to John.

"I-I can't stay here. Not for a week without anyone knowing where I am. I need to make some calls."

Mikaela was getting agitated.

"No calls," said John.

"What do you mean, no calls?" she said, her voice rising.

"Exactly what you heard, no calls, no going outside. No contact outside of me and Masami. The alternative is you get found and most likely erased." said John.

John was losing his patience and took a deep breath as he turned to inspect the space.

"Masami, why don't you explain it to her while I get us situated." said John.

He stepped further into the loft space as Masami turned to speak to an upset Mikaela. He could hear their voices behind him as he walked over to the kitchen area where a laptop was resting on a counter. The loft was divided into a kitchen area, common area and two bedrooms just off the common area.

Sitting on a stool by the kitchen counter, he powered up the laptop and tried to assess the events of the last few hours. Someone was killing assets. Fujita Sensei was killed by his own clan. Mikaela, who was a liability he needed to get rid of, worked for some unknown group and thought he killed Fujita. Masami, another liability as far as he was concerned was determined to "assist" him in anything he attempted to do.

It was a mess. Somehow he needed to straighten this out before he was implicated further and killed. Oh and he still had Trevor to consider, the clock was ticking.

He could hear them speaking. Mikaela's short clipped words sounding like rapid gunfire countered by Masami's easy cadence. He hoped Mikaela would understand, but he knew the type. She was going to be a problem. After checking the space, he came back to the common area.

Mikaela looked straight at him.

"Let me send one email. I can encrypt it. They won't know its point of origin. You don't realize what will be set in motion if my people think I'm dead." said Mikaela.

John thought it over while Masami went to the kitchen to prepare some tea.

"Can you guarantee it won't be traced back here?"

John didn't like it, but if it meant she would cooperate then it was worth it.

"Absolutely, my skills may be a bit rusty but I was one of the best."

"Masami, your thoughts?" said John.

Masami turned to face John.

"She will attempt it regardless." Masami said, as she looked at Mikaela. "Better we know and let her do it now than have to tie her up for a week." said Masami.

John turned to face Mikaela.

"Fine, send your email. Understand that if it's not encrypted at the highest level, we will have visitors, and they won't be your people." said John. "Masami, make sure she is as good as she says."

Mikaela sat at the counter in front of the laptop. Her fingers flew over the keys. After a few minutes, she stood up, apparently finished.

"Thank you." said Mikaela as she sat in the common area, still feeling her injuries.

"You're welcome but just in case." John picked up his phone and dialed.

"Did you get it?" John asked Mole.

"Got it," he said as he chewed.

"Two messages, one straight email and one short burst transmission. She is very good though. I almost didn't see it." said Mole.

John turned to look at Mikaela. She looked at him, defiance in her eyes.

"Who is that?" said Mikaela

"Sanitize the email and send it without the burst transmission." said John.

He looked at Mikaela. She looked away.

"You think this is some game?" asked John.

Mikaela turned to face John; there was no fear in her eyes.

"Look, all I know is you two are responsible or at least involved in the death of one of our assets. For all I know, you killed him." said Mikaela pointing at John.

"Sure that's why I dragged you out of a burning building, because my remorse at killing Fujita Sensei was so great that it drove me to save you." said John.

Mikaela turned to face him, ice in her voice.

"I don't know why you dragged me out of there. I will tell you what I do know. You were at the wrong place at the wrong time. Gustav is more than likely dead and you are holding me here against my will."

Chapter Twenty One

Kei sped across the dojo floor, not using all of her ability, but moving faster than any untrained human could. Lea stood there waiting. *This was going to be too easy*, thought Kei. She bore down on Lea and unleashed a devastating punch at her midsection.

Kei pulled it a bit, after all she didn't want to send her to the hospital, just return the favor and send Lea flying, doubled over in pain would be the bonus. As she completed her technique, the air around Lea shimmered and Kei connected, with nothing.

As Kei turned, Lea slammed a low kick into Kei's left thigh. It was faster than she could register. The muscle spasmed, but she stayed upright. Lea had shifted two feet to her right, causing Kei to miss and overextend herself. The low kick was considered an equalizing technique. It usually stopped an opponent cold.

Kei tested the leg and stepped back a bit. It hurt, but pain was just another sensation like cold or heat. She was aware of the leg but it wasn't going to slow her down.

"You're strong," said Lea.

"You have no idea," Kei answered.

"Let's find out," said Lea as she turned to face Kei.

Chapter Twenty-Two

"Gustav is dead." said John.

Mikaela lowered her head. "He was a good partner, one of the best."

John decided not to tell her that he died protecting her from the blast.

"My absence won't go unnoticed. You probably have a team looking for you right outside this place, wherever we are." Mikaela said as she glanced around at the windows. They were all covered with a frosted film, allowing in light but obscuring detail.

"Your people are the least of my worries." said John.

"Really, my people are pretty good." said Mikaela

"We're jamming any tracking signal you may be transmitting, including your subdermals." said Masami.

Shit, thought Mikaela. *Who were these people?*

"Anyway that's not the issue right now." said John.

"My kidnapping is not an issue, really?" said Mikaela.

"It boggles the mind how you don't see the bigger picture here." said John.

"Enlighten me. Why not start with who you work for. You have company written all over you." said Mikaela.

"I don't work for anyone in alphabet city." said John.

"Convince me."

"I'm guessing this tough as nails act must really scare the people you work with or those who work for you. Around here it's meaningless." said John.

"It's not an act. It is going to be my life's mission to stop you. That, you can believe." said Mikaela as she pointed a finger at John.

John smiled. He was actually starting to like her.

"I do, it's your dance, and you do it any way you feel like. Like I was saying, CATT isn't the main issue here. Someone is killing assets –" started John.

"Yes, you," Mikaela interrupted.

"No, not me." said John. "It's someone with a special skill."

"What kind of skill?" asked Mikaela.

"I don't think sharing that information would be prudent right now." said John.

"You want to say classified, don't you?"

"Let's just say it's not a good idea to share that right now."

"OK, let's pretend it's not you. Where did this mystery person acquire this skill?" said Mikaela.

"I don't know, but that would be the right question to ask."

John pulled out his phone to call Mole. He looked at Masami, indicated she should keep an eye on Mikaela. He went to the bedroom, to avoid being overheard.

"Mole." said John

"Hey, what's up - is everything OK?"

"As OK as can be expected. I need you to do a search on the Fujita family specifically if any are running a martial arts school. It would be obscure, off the beaten path and almost impossible to find." said John.

"You mean impossible for mere mortals, not me, right?"

"Let me know when you find something."

"Got it." said Mole as he hung up.

John came back to the main room to find Mikaela gone and Masami on the floor unconscious.

Going after her would be pointless; it was obvious she was skilled and determined. He gently lifted Masami from the floor and placed her on the sofa. She came to slowly.

"Masami, what happened?" John asked as he handed her a glass of water.

"I underestimated her skill. I turned for a moment. That's the last thing I remember." said Masami.

"She must be quite skilled." said John.

"Indeed." said Masami. She was rubbing her neck and massaging parts of her shoulder.

"We need to leave, now." Masami nodded and tried to stand. She was a little shaky on her feet.

"Do you think you can make it to the car?" said Masami.

"I'll be fine, give me two minutes."

"That's going to be a literal two minutes. We are gone in 120." John went to retrieve the rapid deploy bags he kept in every safe location. The set up was costly but it made leaving a location under stress easy. He checked the contents of both bags and checked his watch. One minute left. He swung by the kitchen, picked up the laptop and placed it in one of the bags. Then he picked up the phone and dialed Mole.

"What's the deal?"

"Cleaning crew, now." said John.

"No, what, are you kidding? I just got that place for you!" said Mole.

"Mikaela is gone. I'll give you details later."

John hung up on Mole, who was getting quite creative with the curses, John noted.

"Time to go, Masami." said John.

"I'm ready," she said as she grabbed the backpack he handed her and slung it over her shoulders.

"Are you sure you're ok?"

She nodded and looked him in the eyes.

"Hai, we don't have time in any case. We must assume this location is compromised." said Masami.

They made it to the car without difficulty. John pressed his finger to the handle and the door opened. John threw his bag in the back seat. He would have to sweep the car for any tracking devices, but time was against him. He pulled out of the garage and headed towards the BQE. He drove assuming he was being followed.

Inside the Essex restaurant Mikaela sat watching as they left.

"You got them?" said Mikaela.

"Copy that, we got them." A voice answered in her earpiece.

"A simple yes or no will do."

Mikaela hated these gung ho types.

"Yes ma'am, picking up their signal clearly."

"Good." she said.

Mikaela was in a foul mood, first having to engineer her own escape and then being sent a second string squad. David was going to hear about this right after she made sure someone paid for this incompetence.

"Um, Ma'am?" said the voice.

"Yes?" she said losing her patience.

"Won't they sweep the car for any tracking device you may have placed?"

"If he has any skill, yes. Keep me updated on their location." she said.

She anticipated his sweeping the car which is why she reconfigured the laptop to be the tracking device. As long as he kept it with him she would know where he was.

I am going to burn you John Kane, she thought as she watched the car pull away.

Chapter Twenty Three

Kei shifted her weight onto her right leg and snapped a side kick at Lea. Lea slid back just out of range, the kick missing by an inch.

"Nice kick," said Lea

Before Kei could react Lea turned her body, snapping her hips. As she completed the turn, she extended her arm, driving a spinning back fist at Kei's head. Kei ducked at the last possible second, the strike barely registered on her radar. If it wasn't for her training, she would be unconscious now, wondering what happened.

"I almost connected. Are you distracted?" said Lea.

What the hell? How can she be so fast? thought Kei.

"Fine, you want pain, I have plenty for you." said Kei.

"All I hear are words, but not much action backing them up." said Lea.

Kei's face reddened. Lea smiled as she took a step back.

"Whenever you are ready, please bring me the pain, if you think you can," said Lea.

Kei inhaled sharply and attacked. She launched a driving front thrust kick that Lea side stepped. She followed that with a devastating low kick designed to break the femur. Lea stepped inside the kick and jammed it, taking the energy of the kick and continuing its circular path by sweeping Kei and throwing her off feet. Kei recovered instantly, planting her feet and unleashing an elbow at Lea's head. Lea ducked and shot an arm into the elbow strike, effectively locking Kei's arm mid-strike. With her free hand, she punched Kei in the solar plexus, forcing the air from her body. Lea retracted the fist and struck Kei along the temple with a knife hand. Kei stood dazed for a second. Lea chambered her hand to strike again, not believing that Kei was still standing, when Kei collapsed in her arms.

"Yame-Stop!" said a voice from the corner of the dojo. It was Himara Sensei.

"Hai Sensei." Lea carried Kei over to the side of the dojo and laid her down. She stepped over to the where Himara Sensei had just sat.

"What do you see?" asked Himara. Lea sat in the formal posture called seiza and bowed.

"May I speak freely Sensei?" said Lea.

"Of course." said Himara.

Lea exhaled slowly as the Sensei sat at a right angle to her.

"She is skilled, highly skilled. Yet she has not mastered her ability. She is not of the bloodline but exhibits one of the five skills of our clan. She is immature and was easily goaded by my remarks into making a fatal error. I would say her training is halfway completed if I had to assess her skill. Whoever trained her knew what they were doing, but left the task incomplete."

Lea bowed when she finished speaking.

The Sensei appeared to have his eyes closed.

"You had several opportunities to end the exchange before this. Why did you not take them?" said Himara.

Lea bowed again. "Each of those opportunities would have caused irreparable harm or a catastrophic failure in one or more of her body's systems. I was under the impression this was a training and assessment exercise."

Sensei Himara nodded slightly.

"Very well, take her to one of the rooms while I consider her future." said Himara.

Lea bowed and paused wanting to speak.

"Sensei?" said Lea.

"Yes?" said Himara.

Himara appeared distracted by thought. He turned to face Lea.

"May I inquire what you intend to do with her?"

The Sensei looked at her for a few moments. Lea felt the full weight of his presence. She was about to apologize when he looked away, his face unreadable.

"As of this moment, my instinct says to wait and see what ripples she has set in motion. This Kei is quite the paradox. On occasion, situations like this do not have immediate answers and it is best to allow them to present us with the solution." said Himara.

"So you don't know," said Lea.

The Sensei laughed then.

"In all your years, you were always the direct one. No, I do not know, daughter. Please take her to a room and see to her injuries." said Himara.

"Hai Sensei."

Lea lifted Kei and made her way to the living quarters. She looked back to see the Sensei, her father still sitting in seiza as immobile as a statue, his presence filling the dojo floor until she felt him everywhere. She looked down at the unconscious Kei and wondered what brought her to their lives and who had taught her the skill she had. An uneasy feeling gripped her stomach. Somehow she knew this was not going to end well.

Chapter Twenty Four

Failure was not an option. It never was. Most who knew him or of him thought his name was Kage, not realizing that it was an honorific, a title. To become the Kage meant he was the most ruthless, skilled and determined of the Shadow Blades. It meant he had fought and killed his way to the top. It also meant he was a prime target. Any blade could challenge the Kage as long as they accepted the terms of the challenge.

Every challenge was a fight to the death. The more skilled the Kage, the less challengers he faced. This Kage had only received one challenge in his two years as leader of the Shadow Blades. He remembered it vividly. The challenge was issued in the traditional manner through a second. It was early in his leadership. The challenger felt that he had ascended to the leadership of the Blades because of his name.

Keiji Fujita realized that to maintain his position he would have to answer the challenge. His challenger was Masato, one of the most skilled Blades.

Masato felt he had a legitimate claim to the leadership of the Blades. Keiji did not question the challenge. He knew he had to beat Masato decisively to firmly establish his leadership. Masato, ten years Keiji's senior had the reputation of being fearsome with the katana. All the arrangements had been made and on the appointed day, they stood before each other. All of the Blades were in attendance as well as three of the clan heads. Masato stood, sword in hand, ready for the victory he knew was assured him. Keiji stood before Masato, calm and serene. Keiji was prepared to die, Masato was not and this made all the difference.

In the end, Keiji dealt honorably with Masato, executing the killing blow with such velocity that Masato didn't register the cut until he tried to move and his head slid off his neck. That was the last challenge Keiji had encountered, until now.

The Blade never left witnesses or survivors, until today. Today two had escaped him. It was a sign of weakness he would not, could not tolerate. This brought him to the present moment. The Blades assigned the task of sanitizing the property stood before him.

"You were instructed to sanitize the location." said Kage.

"Yes, but –" began the first Blade.

The action was too fast to follow. With a flick of his wrist, Kage cut across the Blade's neck. A thin line formed as the blade reached up to his neck in a futile motion. Moments later, he collapsed, dead, blood pooling around the body.

"As I was saying, you were instructed to sanitize the location and you failed." said Kage.

"Yes, Sir, my life is forfeit." His arm had stopped bleeding long before but he knew his life could end in any moment.

The Blade dropped to one knee, head bowed, exposing his neck.

"Your life has always been forfeit, but you will do one last task for me before I claim what is mine." said Kage.

He reached into his shirt pocket and took out two pictures.

"Find them and kill them, then I will give you the death you deserve."

The Blade bowed deeper.

"Thank you Kage."

Kage tossed the pictures on the floor. Even in the low light conditions, the images of Masami and John holding Mikaela as they escaped the burning property were clear.

Chapter Twenty Five

John headed into Queens, an uneasy feeling in his stomach. Mikaela's escape worked in his favor. It allowed him greater freedom. In the long term, having her out there, hunting him was not acceptable. At some point they would cross paths again. She would have to be neutralized somehow.

"She will need to be dealt with." said Masami.

John looked at her quickly.

"It is the most prudent course of action." said Masami.

"I know, I know I was just thinking the same thing," said John.

Masami nodded.

"That will happen soon enough. I don't think she is going on vacation any time soon." said John.

"Do not make my mistake, John. Do not underestimate her." said Masami.

John was about to answer when his phone rang.

"What's the status?" said John.

"Cleaning crew is on site and you were never there. You need to sweep the car, or better yet call Iris and get another vehicle."

"I will. Any more progress on CATT?"

"That's going to take some digging. This place makes a black ops outfit look like its advertising, that's how deep they are. You sure you want me to go after them?" said Mole.

"Can you do it without getting caught?"

"Normally I would say, absolutely, with my eyes closed. But these guys aren't the usual. There is a chance they can trace me."

John had never heard Mole be so cautious. If he was saying it was going to be difficult, it meant CATT had some very skilled people working for them.

"Well, if you can't –" started John.

"Hold on a sec, I didn't say I couldn't. I said there is a chance, slim as it may be, it's there."

John smiled; he knew Mole couldn't back down from a challenge.

"What are you telling me, Mole?"

"I'll get the info, you deal with any backlash."

"Don't I always?" said John.

"Yes you do."

"Anything else you have for me?" said John.

"Yep, found a location for you regarding the Fujita martial arts school. They're off the beaten path, hard to find, kind of exclusive. They don't advertise or promote themselves.

"If they are that hard to find, how did you find them?" asked John.

"John, John, John. I'm insulted. I merely put my demi god powers to good use." said Mole.

"Right your lordship. Do you have an address?"

"I'm getting the distinct impression that my near divinity is being questioned."

"The address?" said John.

"I sent it to your phone."

"Good. Let me know when you make progress on CATT. Mikaela won't hang back for too long. I want to be prepared."

"I'm on it. Be careful with the ice queen, John. I'll put a folder together on her for you as well. It's going to be thin though."

"Thanks, Mole." John hung up.

John looked at the address and saw it was in Williamsburg, Brooklyn. The area had recently been invaded by a wave of young professionals and the developers had capitalized on it. New construction was everywhere. Old industrial buildings were being converted into condos and lofts. The old neighborhood John recalled was a distant memory.

"Where are we going?" asked Masami.

"To see if we can get some answers," John said as he headed for the exit that would lead him into the heart of Brooklyn.

Chapter Twenty Six

Trevor was not prone to nervousness. He had faced situations that had undone many of his colleagues. It wasn't that he was fearless. He knew better than that. Rather he accepted fear, embraced and expected it. To Trevor, fear was a comfortable garment, form fitting and snug. He had grown accustomed to it and it had lost its power over him. He was a highly trained asset and yet none of his training removed the unease he felt in the pit of his stomach.

He told the director that involving Kane was an error. He still felt that John should have been eliminated while they had the opportunity. That window was all but closed. Now inadvertently or not, CATT was involved. He would have to deal with the team led by Petrovich who was like a dog with a bone. She would not relent

90

until forced to. It was getting more complicated by the hour. Sooner rather than later, he would have to take the necessary steps to ensure there was no blowback from this op. He was going to have to get his hands dirty.

He hated getting his hands dirty.

Chapter Twenty Seven

Kei's body approached consciousness cautiously. Her body ached everywhere and her return to awareness was reluctant as if her body knew what was waiting. She looked around; she was in someone's bedroom.

"Oh good, you're awake. Sorry about the room. Sensei wanted you here so you wouldn't attract too much attention. Are you feeling better?"

The voice was familiar to Kei, but she still felt like she was in a dream state. Then it all came rushing back, the voice belonged to the woman who had put her in this state to begin with - Lea.

Kei carefully took in the room, noticing the sparseness of furniture or personal items. Lea saw her looking around and answered her question.

"This used to be my old bedroom, when I lived here. Now it's given to visiting Sensei or guests of the school. We don't really get many of either, so it goes mostly unused." said Lea.

Kei was upset and remained quiet. Lea picked up on her mood.

"I can see you're upset, what I don't understand is why. It was your fault," said Lea.

"My fault – ow!" Kei tried sitting up.

"I wouldn't make any sudden moves if I were you." said Lea.

Kei settled back down into the bed.

"How is what happened my fault?" said Kei.

Kei moved slowly around the throbbing pain in her head.

"Your first mistake was holding back in the beginning. In a life and death context, you would be dead. You never hold back when facing a superior enemy. Mistake one. You failed to recognize you were facing a superior enemy which would have been evident if emotion did not cloud your decision making process. Mistake Two. You let me goad you into making amateur errors. You were as easy to read as a book.

I was able to use that and maneuver you where I wanted. You didn't see the fight took place on several levels. The physical level was only the most apparent. Mistake three. If you add all that, had I been intent on killing you, would have been very dead. Frankly I'm surprised you have made it this far."

Lea sat back and waited. Kei slumped back quiet, realizing Lea was right.

Chapter Twenty Eight

Williamsburg was quiet at night. There was the usual activity but John could tell it was subdued. He had wanted to go to the address at night to get a feel for the place. The dojo was in a nondescript building.

If he didn't have the address Mole had given him, he wouldn't have found it. He drove around twice, once wide, the other narrow and then parked several blocks away. After parking he did another circuit, of the area on foot just to be certain he hadn't attracted any attention. So far he and Masami were alone. He knew it wouldn't last. The car was a serious liability. He took out his phone as he stood a few blocks from the corner of the address Mole gave him.

"Mole." said John.

"Hey John, find the place?" asked Mole.

"The last thing this place looks like is a dojo."

"I would imagine that's the point, no?"

"I know what you are thinking and that is the place that fits the description you gave me. Only way to know for sure would be to, oh I don't know, go in?" said Mole.

"Fair enough," said John.

"Do you need anything else? Some of us like to sleep."

"Yes, call Iris. Have her track the vehicle, perform a sweep and I need a replacement, something a little more common with the same load out. Make it American." said John.

"American are you sure?" said Mole.

"Absolutely and forgettable." said John.

"Something like a minivan?" Mole laughed.

"If Iris shows up with a minivan –"

"I know, I know, I'll see what I can do." said Mole.

"Let me know if the sweep turns up anything. If it isn't on the car then I have to consider other options."

"You can start with the laptop." said Mole.

"The thought has crossed my mind but it may be put to good use if it is the laptop."

"Your call. I'll let you know when Iris arrives."

"Thanks," said John and hung up.

John turned to Masami who had been standing next to him.

"Now we wait." said John.

Chapter Twenty Nine

"Shit." whispered Kei.

She had been played like a rank amateur.

"Shit indeed." said Lea. "You need to finish your training. I won't lie to you. You have a lot of ability."

"But?" said Kei.

"But it's like you're half done." said Lea after a moment. She looked at Kei gauging her reaction. Kei turned away, the pain making her wince. Lea placed a bowl of hot broth and a cup of pungent tea on the table beside Kei's bed.

"Ugh what is that?" said Kei. The smell made her nauseous.

"Both of these will help you heal and restore your strength." said Lea.

"I have to really drink that?" said Kei.

"Yes now. Drink up." said Lea.

She waited patiently for Kei to begin. Kei began with the broth. When Lea was satisfied she had drunk enough of both she reached into the bag she carrying.

"Feel better?" said Lea.

"No I don't, this soup tastes like someone's idea of a prank." said Kei.

Lea laughed.

"That's about how I remember it too." said Lea.

"In any case, you're in no condition to go anywhere today. You need to heal. Why don't you do something productive while you're getting back on your feet?" said Lea.

Lea placed a book on the bed beside Kei.

"What's this?" said Kei.

It was a worn journal, the pages yellowed with age.

"That is a family journal. It should help you. Read it, learn it. It doesn't usually get read by someone outside of the family. Sensei must think you have real potential if he is letting you see it." said Lea.

Kei shifted in the bed through clenched teeth as the pain radiated in her body.

Lea noticed the grimace and smiled.

"Don't worry you should feel better by tomorrow morning. That broth tastes horrible but works miracles." said Lea.

"Please tell Sensei I said thank you." said Kei after she adjusted enough to be comfortable.

Lea stood to leave and bowed. "I will."

Kei turned to the first page of the journal and read:

After many days of sitting and meditation we were able to direct our energies in truly unimaginable ways. These abilities border on the impossible, but I am assured by our Sensei that they are perfectly within the realm of this world, though many fail to achieve the state required to draw or manifest this energy. This does not mean that it does not exist.

Sensei also alluded to certain family traits that may make entering this state easier. When I asked him if it was only our family, he answered as only he could, saying the Fujita line was not particularly special, just very determined.

The inception of the skills is open to all who pursue them wholeheartedly. Their mastery is quite another matter. Train hard and persevere - those are the keys.

Kei closed the journal and placed it next to her on the bed. She was still sore and it hurt to move. She was conflicted. Part of her wanted to run, like she did so many years ago. She knew her Sensei must have had a reason for having her come here, maybe this was it. Besides she couldn't leave until told to. Begrudgingly she had to admit that Lea was right. She needed to finish her training. She thought back to the fight between her and Lea and grimaced. Lea had handled her so easily. She could feel the anger rising.

Is this why her Sensei had sent her here? So she could finish her training?

Calm down, she thought and took a deep breath. She finished the broth and the tea and settled back in bed, placing the journal on the side table. She was suddenly exhausted and her eyes felt heavy.

She would finish her training, do whatever it took.

Then she would kick Lea's ass all over the dojo floor. With that thought, she fell asleep.

Chapter Thirty

The sun blazed across the sky, casting an orange fire over the city. Dawn was John's favorite part of the day. For him it was rebirth. The day held possibility. It was unformed, a blank slate waiting to be written upon, created.

"If this is a traditional dojo," John mused, "there will be some kind of morning class."

"We just have to wait for the students to arrive." said Masami.

As the sun cast its light over the horizon, Masami stood silently beside him. They didn't have to wait long. A few minutes later, several people entered the building, each carrying some sort of bag or backpack. Masami placed a hand on John's arm.

"We must tread carefully here Kane -san, those are not ordinary students." John agreed, he didn't know how Masami came to her conclusion, but years of being around highly trained individuals let him know these were not ordinary students. He read the posture, the walk, the intent. Each of the six people that entered, men and women, were well trained. He didn't want them to think they were dojo storming.

Let's go make a good impression he thought as He made his way across the street, Masami a silent shadow behind him.

John entered the building followed by Masami. The dojo was located on the second floor. John could already hear the familiar sounds, uniforms snapping, feet gliding across the hardwood floors. The smell really brought it home for him. It was the scent peculiar to certain schools. The smell of incense, wood and the hint of sweat never truly dissipate in this kind of school. There were no signs and no exterior indicators that this was a dojo. It seemed like the idea was to dissuade people from joining.

John noticed there was no seating in the reception area. The area was dominated by a large desk, currently unoccupied.

"Must not be many visitors at this hour." said John more to himself than Masami.

"Or any hour it seems." said Masami.

Behind the desk, John could hear the activity on the dojo floor. His view was obscured by a large wooden screen. There was no way to see what occurred on the floor without actually going around the screen and onto the floor. John removed his shoes and peered in; long enough to attract attention, but not enough to be rude.

A young woman in a white uniform entered the reception area. Everything about her said practicality. Her hair was in a tight bun, she wore no make-up. John could see no hint of jewelry. Her uniform was worn from use yet he could tell she starched it. Her movements like the rest of her were economical and efficient. She was about Masami's height and seemed unassuming. She wore a white belt around her waist but John got the impression she was no beginner.

"Good morning," said John as he bowed. "My name is John and this is Masami."

"Good morning, how can I help you?"

"Would it be possible to speak to the Sensei?" asked John.

"May I ask what this pertains to?" she said guardedly.

"It's a private matter." John knew he would be testing his welcome but he wanted to see how many layers there were to the school. The young woman stood silent a moment, looking at the pair before her as if determining to eject them herself.

"Please wait here." she said and re-entered the dojo.

A few moments later, another woman appeared.

"Hello, my name is Lea. I have been informed that you wish to see the Sensei on a private matter?"

"Yes, is he in?" John knew the answer, but asked anyway.

"No, he is not but maybe you can discuss the matter with me. I am his daughter."

John wasn't expecting that.

"My apologies, I don't mean to be rude, but I must discuss this matter only with him." said John.

"I see. Well in that case, you will need to return later today around 1pm. What did you say tour name was again?" said Lea.

"My name is John Kane and this is my assistant Masami."

"Very well, I will let the Sensei know to expect you at 1pm sharp." She emphasized the last word.

"Thank you. I look forward to meeting him."

John bowed and headed for the exit.

"Before you go, who referred you to us? said Lea."

John turned and looked at Lea.

"No one." said John as he left.

Chapter Thirty-One

She followed the asset for several blocks. Her abilities made it easy. Whenever the asset turned to see if he was being followed or shadowed she would simply not be there. It was almost too easy. Then she checked herself. *Don't get complacent and never underestimate your opponent no matter how weak they appear.* The words rushed back to her, words uttered by her long dead teacher. This was the only way to make them pay. The only way they would feel loss like she did. It was a gaping hole in her center that could never be filled. Each asset had given her a piece of the puzzle, the greater whole coming into focus.

She would fulfill her duty and then she could rest. The asset entered a building on Madison Avenue. She checked the address, 760 Madison Avenue. It didn't make sense but then assets usually dealt with covers and shell companies. She entered the building, careful to keep her head down to avoid the cameras. The entire city was being overrun with surveillance. It was just that most people were unaware or apathetic. She didn't know which was worse. She saw the elevator stopped on the tenth floor. She checked the directory and found the tenant to be the Cobalt Design Group.

Unfamiliar but she made a mental note to look it up later. She pressed the call button and waited. The building was at least eighty years old with a nod to the art deco design that was popular during its construction.

A minute later, the elevator dinged and the doors slid open. She stepped in and pressed ten. She really disliked being in elevators. Moving caskets, that's what they were called when she was younger. *Always take the stairs, on a flight of stairs you have options. In an elevator all you can do is react and usually die.* The ever present voice of her teacher reminded her.

The elevator being much newer than the building arrived at the tenth floor without incident. As she got off, she realized Cobalt Design occupied the entire floor. She knocked on the door and found it unlocked. Every fiber of her being urged her to turn and walk away but she knew it wasn't an option. If this was a trap and she was fairly certain it was, there was only one way she would exit this building.

She had to spring the trap.

She pushed open the door slowly half expecting gunfire to erupt.

"Come in please." The voice, a deep baritone, emanated from somewhere nearby. The floor of the office space was mostly empty.

"Looks like Cobalt Design has hit a rough patch." she said.

"We keep various locations throughout the city. It suits our purposes from time to time." the voice said.

"We?" she said.

She could sense others in the space with her.

'Yes, we-I am afraid your search comes to an end here. Kill her."

Chapter Thirty-Two

Mikaela had tracked John to some nondescript neighborhood in Brooklyn when she got the call. She looked at her phone, cursed and for a second considered letting it go to voicemail, then thought better of it. David only called if it was important.

"Yes David," she said as she picked up.

"I need you to pay me a visit." said David.

Even though it sounded like a request, Mikaela knew better. She also knew better than to argue.

"When?" she asked, hoping to buy some time. She wanted to pin down John before he found the tracking device in the laptop.

"Now," he said in a soft spoken voice.

"I can't do now." *Or the next few days* she thought to herself.

"It can't be helped. It was either this or pull you from the field. You don't have many friends in CATT Mika. There are a few of the opinion that you should be retired, permanently." said David.

This didn't surprise or even annoy her. She knew many felt this way about her, more importantly she knew who they were. She also knew David supported her completely, which was part of the reason she was untouchable. The other part was that she lived up to and exceeded her reputation. Mikaela was not the kind of enemy you wanted to fight, on any battlefield.

"Fine, David. Where would you like to meet?" she said exasperated.

He hated leaving the compound so she thought this would buy her a few hours at least.

"I'll be at this location in forty minutes; I'm sending the address to your phone. I'll meet you there." said David.

Mikaela was too surprised to answer. David never made what he liked to call 'house calls'.

"Oh and I'm bringing your new partner. Her name is Helen. Helen Martine."

He hung up before Mikaela could answer. The shock had rendered her speechless.

Chapter Thirty-Three

It wasn't the first time she had been underestimated. She didn't know if it was because she was a woman or of slight build. The office space of Cobalt Design was sparsely furnished and now she knew why. This was a place where people disappeared.

"Kill her and make sure there is no trace of her being here," the voice said.

At least she knew she was on the right track. She just had to get out of this alive.

She sensed there were ten others, probably armed. When they stepped out of the shadows, she cursed to herself.

Shit. Shadow Blades. This was going to be messy. She took a breath to center herself. *Divide and destroy when outnumbered. Each strike must count.* Her master's lesson came back to her. She slid to the nearest wall to prevent getting surrounded, knowing that would be fatal.

A Shadow Blade advanced - his short sword down. She focused on the immediate threat but kept her awareness large in case they charged. It seemed this was the leader of this group. Men and their egos, they always had something to prove. It would have been smarter to attack en masse but since there was only one of her, what threat could she pose?

She could almost see the thought process. They would attack as a group after this. She remained still and let him advance. Her stillness was considered unnatural. She could remain motionless almost indefinitely. Its effect caused her opponents to attack, giving her the opening she needed. She waited for the Shadow Blade to strike. He drew closer. She could sense the incoming lunge but she didn't move. He took a gliding step forward and thrust this blade at her midsection.

At the last possible moment, she twisted her torso. The blade caught in the fabric of her shirt, which was the intention. She kept the rotation going, snagging the blade and drawing him in. As she turned, she brought her hand down in a shuto-knife edge strike, using the edge of her hand on his wrist. She instantly shattered all the bones in his wrist. Shock and surprise registered on his face. She let it sit for a moment as he let go of his blade, his hand no longer functional. She grabbed the short sword and he knew what was next. She saw the acceptance, the certainty in his eyes. As she pulled it from her tangled shirt, she sliced across his neck in one smooth motion. He fell to the ground, his life pouring out of him. Five seconds had passed.

The other Shadow Blades recovered quickly, but it was too late. She was in motion. She blurred behind the nearest one and stabbed him through the heart. Turning him to receive the blow that came from her right, she kicked that Shadow Blade in the knee, destroying it. As he fell to the ground, she grabbed his neck and broke it.

Seven more, ten seconds had passed.

She ducked under the slice of one sword, punching as she did so. Her fist broke through his rib cage and crushed his heart. He crumpled to the ground. The next two attacked together, she slid away from one thrust and twisted away from the other as she launched two daggers burying them in the necks of both. They fell, surprise in their eyes.

Four to go, twenty seconds passed.

She walked to the center of the floor and let them surround her now. The attack came as she anticipated and she let it. Four swords thrust at her and bounced off her body. She back fisted the Shadow Blade in front of her crushing his skull and killing him instantly. She grabbed the throat of the one on her left and ripped his larynx from his neck. The one on her right was about to step back when she drove her fingertips into his neck slicing through his jugular.

One left, behind her. Thirty seconds passed.

"You have a choice," she said without turning around. "You can go back to your Master, report what occurred here and receive death at his hand, or die here."

He drew a second weapon, making his choice.

"I understand," she said as she turned. She blurred before he could react and placed a palm on his chest giving a slight push and exploding his heart.

Forty five seconds had passed.

Chapter Thirty-Four

John realized that telling him to come back at one was a delay tactic. He expected they thought he was dojo storming at best or meant their Sensei harm at worst. In any case, he knew he could expect to face off against several seniors if he wanted to speak to the Sensei. He and Masami returned at a quarter to one. The young woman from earlier in the morning was behind the desk. As she looked up, a brief moment of surprise crossed her face as if she didn't expect to see them again. She nodded slightly to John and pressed a button on her desk. Moments later, one of the largest men John had seen in a long time, came into the waiting area.

"This is Terence," the woman at the desk said. "He will take you to the changing area so you can prepare."

Terence bowed and in that one motion, John could ascertain the high level of skill he possessed. Terence turned and entered the dojo. John followed. He was led to a back room that served as a changing area and part storage. There were no lockers but small cubbies covered one side wall. A few benches were in the center of the floor, allowing for ease of changing. Terence reached into one of the cubbies and produced a worn white uniform. He held it out for John.

"Clothes in there," he pointed at the cubby. "When you're ready, you go out this way," he pointed to another doorway that led to the dojo area, at least that's what the sign on the door said.

John nodded 'Thank you' and began to disrobe.

"Are you sure you want to do this?" said Terrance.

John paused a moment as he was changing.

"Is there another way to speak alone with the Sensei?" John asked.

Terrence looked at John and shook his head slowly.

"Not really. Sensei doesn't get many visitors these days." said Terrence.

"I understand. It's not that kind of dojo." said john.

"No it isn't. The students you will be facing won't take it easy on you. It's not personal. It's just the way it is."

John nodded and kept disrobing. He understood the need for this, especially since he requested to speak to the Sensei alone. Terrence waited while he changed into the uniform that was provided. John headed to the door that indicated the dojo area. He turned to Terrence who bowed.

"See you on the floor." said Terrence.

John wasn't surprised that Terrence would be one of his opponents. He bowed. "See you there."

The dojo did surprise John. It was a spacious area without columns. He had trained in a few schools similar to this one. The ceremonial center, the shomen held the only scroll. It read Ren Ma, Zanshin, Mushin and Fudoshin. John was familiar with the concepts but he had never seen it in a school depicted as such.

Like most traditional schools, the floor was hardwood and the smell of old wood mixed with sweat was stronger here and brought some pleasant and not so pleasant memories rushing back. Above the scroll work was a small shrine which was a familiar fixture to John. The door he entered had him facing the shomen-the ceremonial center. On his left was a row of students. John guessed they would be in rank order from those lowest, closest to him, to highest closest to the shomen and the sensei.

The sensei or at least, John thought it was the sensei, sat before the shomen area on his knees in the traditional kneeling posture of seiza. John looked to his right and saw that Masami had been seated in an area that was off the dojo floor proper. She was still able to view the entire dojo floor. She looked at John and he could tell she was concerned. He also knew she could not intervene. He was on his own. He took several steps forward and then kneeled in seiza. He bowed, placing his left hand on the floor first, then the right, and then slowly sat up.

"I sincerely thank you for this opportunity. My name is John Kane and you honor me," said John.

The Sensei bowed and signaled to the first student. John stood to meet his first opponent. She stood about five feet tall, with a thin wiry dancer's frame. Her long black hair was tied in a braid and her deep brown eyes were piercing.

She bowed to John.

"My name is Erica Vasquez, second dan and it is you who honor us," she said.

Her belt had no symbols or rankings on it, if she had not told him he would have never known she was a second degree black belt. It seemed rank was not determined by stripes in this school.

The protocol over, John knew they would be anxious to engage him. A second dan was nothing to take lightly. If she was the lowest rank, John couldn't imagine what the last student on the line was. At first glance that last student appeared to be Terrence but beside him, dwarfed and hidden, sat someone else. When John looked closer, he recognized her as Lea, the Sensei's daughter.

Just great, thought John.

"Hajime!" yelled the sensei.

It was the signal to begin. The voice seemed to come from everywhere at once, almost startling John. Erica assumed a left lead fighting stance that John had faced countless times. He knew they would be looking for any weaknesses or chinks in his defense. He had decided not to use his ability to blur, since it would give him an unfair advantage, which was part honor and part ego. He wanted to see if he could do this without having to blur. It was mostly ego.

Erica glided in and launched a side kick meant to break anything it came in contact with. John barely sidestepped the leg only to have to block a descending elbow.

Using a modified rising block, rather than meeting force with force, he received the elbow and redirected the energy, pulling the elbow down as he stepped back, forcing Erica to one knee. As she went down, he stepped around her, locking the elbow and placing her in a headlock. As he began to apply pressure she began to shift her weight, but he was waiting for that. Adjusting his stance, he applied more pressure until he was sure she was unconscious. Erica was going to wake up with one hell of a headache but she would wake up.

Several students who were not part of the line came and collected Erica, taking her off the dojo floor. The next student stood and stepped towards John. He bowed, John returned the bow. No names or ranks were exchanged. From here on, it would only be fighting until John beat them all or was defeated.

Chapter Thirty-Five

Mikaela hated partners. It wasn't a personal thing. David usually gave her the best to work with. It's just that her operative style - for lack of a better term, made it difficult. Being highly intelligent, she didn't suffer fools lightly and David knew that. So she knew her new partner would at least rate off the charts in intelligence. Not that it always helped. It wasn't enough they were intelligent, they needed to be savvy, they needed to be adaptable, survivors. Mikaela sighed; she didn't have a choice.

She walked down the block from the makeshift base of operations David had set up located on Franklin Street. As she waited on the corner of Broadway and Franklin, a black Range Rover pulled up. She was mildly surprised to see the lone vehicle, expecting an entourage of trucks. The tinted window on the driver's side lowered and David peered at her.

"Hello Mika." said David.

She remained stone-faced, indicating that she was not pleased.

"I know, Mika, just get in," said David.

She got in the Rover and sat across from David in the passenger side. In the back seat sat Helen. At least she assumed it was Helen. David turned to face Mikaela.

"How are you?" said David.

"I'm fine David, aside from the wet behind the ears squad you gave me –" began Mikaela.

"It was the best I could do on short notice."

David held up his hand to stop her response.

"Hear me out. Mika." said David.

Mikaela sat back and looked at Helen, who only stared out of the window as if she were in the vehicle alone. Mikaela turned to face David again, cocking her head in askance about Helen's aloofness.

"I'll get to that in a second. First let me say my piece then I will make intros. You, Mikaela are very hard on partners and my nerves. I thought Gustav would make the cut, obviously I was mistaken. You need to wrap up this Kane business, ASAP." Mikaela made to speak and David glared.

"There are things occurring that you are not privy to Mika. In order to facilitate a speedy resolution to your current situation, I'm giving you a new partner. Mikaela meet Helen Martine."

Helen turned then and looked at Mikaela. She had close cropped hair bordering on a screaming eagle military cut. Her green eyes took in Mikaela as if assessing what kind of threat she would be.

"Hello," Helen said. Her voice was clear and direct without an accent, at least not one Mikaela could detect.

Mikaela nodded and turned to David.

"No offense to my new partner here, but what makes her qualified to join me in the field?" said Mikaela.

Helen turned abruptly to look out her window. She pulled out what appeared to be a 9mm Glock. Mikaela reached for her own weapon.

"What the hell? David?" said Mikaela.

"David," Helen said in an even tone.

"What?" said David as he turned to face Helen.

"Are we expecting anyone else?" said Helen.

"Not that I'm aware of. Why?"

"I thought as much, you may want to tell them." she said as she pointed out the window. David turned in time to see the figure crouch and launch an RPG.

Helen had rolled out of the vehicle ending on one knee and firing her silenced weapon, hitting the crouched man holding the RPG launcher. David and Mikaela had both cleared the vehicle in time to see it go up in an explosion. David pulled out two desert eagles and Mikaela drew her modified Glock 20.

"David I'm going to guess they were sent here for me." said Mikaela. "How did they know where we were?"

David looked around, the shadows seemed alive.

"That was just to get us out of the Rover, Mika. We need to move, that's going to attract attention." David said pointing to the Rover. They set off at a brisk pace north towards Canal Street with Helen bringing up the rear.

"Was that for you or me, David?" Mikaela asked as they ran.

"I would put my money on you. Was your team on site?" asked David.

"Shit." Mikaela knew the entire team was now dead.

"Like I said, they are looking for you. The question of the evening is who sent them." said David.

They arrived at Canal and Broadway.

"This is where we split up Mika. You and Helen keep heading north. I will stay here and deal with our new friends," said David.

"Alone? Even if you had enough ammo for ten of those cannons, there are too many variables. This is suicide, you can't take them on alone." said Mikaela, frustration creeping into her voice.

David looked around the deserted intersection of one of the busiest streets in the city.

"Mika, I am never alone." said David.

As if on cue, five of the largest men Mika had seen in her life appeared as if from thin air. One stepped forward.

"Sir we have the area contained and anticipate contact in –" he looked down at his watch, "two minutes, Sir."

"Very good, brief the team. I would like one of them alive if possible. Let's see if we can find out who they are." said David.

Mikaela could barely contain her surprise. David was much more than he let others believe. She made a mental note to not piss him off, too much. Placing an earpiece into his ear, David turned to face Mikaela and Helen. "You two need to go, now. Wrap up this Kane thing. Bring him in and do it fast." he said.

"And where exactly are we going? More importantly how are we going uptown? By subway?" asked Mikaela.

"Helen will brief you on the way," David said as he passed Helen some keys.

"Subway, very funny Mika, like I want to be dealing with city officials asking why the subway is out of commission, which it would be if your friends follow you down. I swear, destruction follows you like a plague. Get out of here and don't get killed." said David.

He turned back to the mountain of a man named Rogers and began coordinating the operation. Helen walked to another Rover parked half a block away, pressed the fob, opened the door and started the truck. Mikaela slid into the passenger side marveling at David's forethought, which came very close to paranoia.

"OK partner, where to?" said Mikaela realizing that her target was in Brooklyn and wouldn't sit still for long.

Helen handed Mikaela a folder.

"David thinks CATT has been compromised, after that little stunt back there I'm inclined to agree, which is why I was brought in. My creds are in there in case you're still curious if I'm qualified," said Helen as she drove north on Broadway.

After seeing her in action, Mikaela didn't need further convincing about Helen's physical ability. It was the mental ability that concerned her the most.

"So we are going? –"asked Mikaela.

"To meet a contact that can help us with the leak at CATT. Then to your target, it seems everything may be connected. At least David thinks so."

They rode on in silence as Mikaela read and Helen drove.

Chapter Thirty Six

John could sense this next student would be more of a challenge than Erica. He could feel the energy emanating from his opponent, the seated students and everyone else in the dojo, except the Sensei. There was an absence of energy where the Sensei sat. John knew this was not coincidental but rather an indicator of the high level of skill the Sensei possessed. It was something to think about later. Right now he had more immediate concerns to deal with. The student before him looked quite muscular. He was slightly taller than John. His face looked as if it was chiseled from stone, his square jaw just showing signs of a shadow. His fists looked around the size of sledge hammers and just as hard. His knuckles were callused from repeated hitting against a hard surface. John felt sorry for whatever he had been hitting.

"Hajime-Begin!" said the Sensei

"Before we start, may I ask your name?" said John.

The student nodded, apparently confident in his ability to dispatch this intruder. With a thick Slavic accent, he said, "My name is Dragan, we begin now."

John dodged a fist the size of subcompact intent on removing his head. Dragan was fast, *almost too fast for his size*, thought John. *Is it possible he is blurring on some level, maybe even unconsciously?* John sidestepped an axe kick that would have broken his collar bone had it landed. It reverberated through the dojo as it hit the floor.

John unleashed several punches to Dragan's midsection, careful not to hit too hard. He actually heard one of the ribs crack. When he looked up at Dragan's face he saw him smile.

"That is good, now we fight for real." He cracked his neck and unleashed a five punch combination. John managed to block and evade four, the fifth punch connected, forcing most of the air out of John's lungs and forcing him back several feet. Unconsciousness hovered at the edges of John's awareness.

Mental note, do not get hit by Dragan again, he thought.

Dragan did not push his advantage confident in the outcome.

Blurring had several facets. It wasn't only the ability to evade and move faster than the eye could follow. When blurring was channeled into a technique, for example, a fist, it had the same effect as a jack hammer, giving the attacker the equivalent of twenty strikes in one blow. John didn't want to kill Dragan, but there was no way he was going to get hit by those cinder blocks he called fists again.

He took a deep breath and opened his hands. The air around his hands began to shimmer. Once he felt centered, John approached. Dragan smiled again, with something close to admiration in his eyes. Apparently not many took a blow from him and continued to fight. John stepped in and to the right, avoiding a vicious left elbow strike. As the elbow grazed John's head, John placed a hand on the triceps, effectively detaching it from its point of insertion. The strain was so great that Dragan's bicep detached as well. John continued sliding to the right and pivoted to face Dragan. Dragan turned to face John.

"What? Come fight me, or are you going to just touch me and run?" said Dragan.

John stood back, knowing what was coming. The pain crashed on Dragan like a relentless wave.

"Ahh! He is armed! What are you carrying you coward?" Dragan stepped back cradling his left arm.

John stood back, hands raised to show he was unarmed.

"Yasime," said the Sensei. It was the command to stop.

Dragan was escorted off the dojo floor. Terrence stood but the Sensei motioned for him to sit, looking at Lea instead. Lea stood and walked to the center of the dojo.

"Thank you for honoring me. Please do not hold back," she said as she bowed.

John took a deep breath and knew this would be the hardest challenge. He bowed to Lea.

"The honor is mine. I request your full commitment as you will have mine." said John.

The protocol was old but basically they had just declared that only one of them would walk away from this fight.

Chapter Thirty Seven

After twenty minutes, Helen pulled up to a townhouse at 1 West Twenty-Second Street.

"This is the address," said Helen as she surveyed the area for hostiles.

Chelsea had changed considerably in the past five years, going from a nondescript neighborhood to a cultural mecca. Galleries had appeared virtually overnight. Mikaela got out and looked around warily.

"Do we have a name?" she asked.

Helen nodded as she closed the driver side door with a small thump.

114

"George Stevens. I don't know how he came by his information but it seems David thinks he is a reliable source so, here we are." said Helen.

Mikaela looked at the townhouse and noted the four floors. The style was turn of the century back when this area was the home of the rich and affluent that preferred not to live on Madison Avenue only a few blocks away.

"What floor is he on?" Mikaela asked as she headed up the steps. She couldn't believe someone with this kind of information would be so exposed.

"Apparently all of them, Stevens owns the building and the one next to it." said Helen.

Mikaela arched an eyebrow.

"Really, I'm guessing George is a trust fund baby, perhaps? What's his background?" said Mikaela.

"Can't say. File on him is so short it's useless, which usually means enough on its own. In my experience dealing with a ghost is bad news, usually ends up biting you in the ass." said Helen.

Mikaela grunted in agreement and pressed the bell for the first floor. She noticed the camera perched in an oblique corner and looked directly at it. The door unlatched moments later. A handsome forty something dressed in jeans and an Armani Exchange T-shirt opened the door. Mikaela checked off the trust fund baby in her head as she noticed the man.

"George, George Stevens?" asked Mikaela.

"Yes, please come in. I've been expecting you. David said you would be dropping by today." said George as he headed back up the winding staircase.

"Really, when was this?" said Mikaela

George stopped a moment on the stairs as if in thought then continued.

"About ten minutes ago. You guys have a real security issue in your organization." said George.

George arrived on the second floor which was a large spacious living/sitting room. Several computers lined one of the walls and Mikaela could tell from glancing at the hardware that they were a hacker's wet dream.

"Some nice equipment you have here." she said as she walked by some of the computers.

"I just dabble here and there, you know nothing too serious," he waved his hand dismissively as he sat down on one of the futons opposite the computer terminals.

Helen turned to face George.

"You have some information for us?" said Helen.

George gestured for them to sit.

"Ah where are my manners? Would you like something to drink, coffee, tea, juice?"

"No thanks." Helen and Mikaela said together.

"So who do you work for?" asked Mikaela.

"I'm mostly freelance but David and I go way back. He asked me to look into this for him; he always had a healthy dose of paranoia. Anyway it turns out your organization or group, CATT, is compromised. God who thinks up these awful acronyms?" said George as he went to a computer.

"Compromised, how?" said Mikaela.

Mikaela felt something was off but couldn't pinpoint it yet. Her gut was telling her not to trust this 'informant'.

"Can you be more specific?" said Helen.

"Sure, one second." He began typing rapidly. "By the way, your security sucks. Well not really," he laughed. "But it has some glaring holes. Ok there." he said as he pointed to the screen.

Mikaela had to read it twice before her brain processed the information. It was a kill order, priority black – the highest level.

"Are you certain this is valid?" said Mikaela in a measured voice, the anger threatening to break free.

Mikaela stepped away and began to think how this would be possible. Helen went over to the screen and read the order.

"Shit," she whispered.

The screen was linked to the CATT's secure system, under the termination heading was one line: *Termination order-Petrovich, Mikaela – Priority Black – Commissioned –Soros, David - Director*

"David ordered this?" asked Mikaela incredulously.

"Doesn't make sense, does it? So the answer would be no," said George.

"So who –"

Mikaela couldn't believe her eyes. This was a serious nightmare in the making. Every available resource would be allocated for her termination. What happened earlier was just the beginning. Mikaela looked at Helen.

"Listen Helen if you –" started Mikaela.

"I don't abandon partners. If David felt you were good enough to be my partner, that's enough for me." said Helen. "Looks like you need me now more than ever."

Mikaela couldn't disagree with her. Mikaela turned to George. She had gotten control of the anger and now appeared to be calm and collected. It was this ability that earned her the name 'ice queen'. She had to assume CATT was operating against her, which explained why David had come to her. She would have been apprehended, detained and summarily erased had she gone to the CATT site. She looked at Helen and knew this was David's way of helping her, providing her with an ally.

"Do you have a secure line I could use to make a call?" asked Mikaela.

"All my lines are secure. Please help yourself. I'm sure he would like to hear from you before he dies." said George.

If Mikaela was surprised, she didn't show it. The fact that George knew she was going to call David wasn't the surprising part. It was the knowledge of the protocol she had discussed with David years earlier. David who always believed in being prepared had told her that if things ever went south at CATT, that she should be ready to "die". He meant it as a figurative death, dropping off the grid and going underground. She chalked it up to his paranoia back then. Nevertheless he made sure she had documents, several false passports, money in accounts and several safe houses to run to should she need to go to ground. She thought he was being excessive, now she whispered a quiet thanks to his neuroses.

She picked up one of the cell phones and dialed David. He picked up on the second ring.

"I see you met my friend." said David.

No names which meant he thought his line was not secure.

"I did. Apparently someone wants me to retire." said Mikaela.

"Not me, but it seems that way."

He was telling her he had nothing to do with her kill order.

"Have my friend show you the other retirement plan. It would seem I'm supposed to join you."

Mikaela looked a question at George, who pointed to the screen in front of him. It was another termination order, this one was for David. It didn't say who ordered it.

"Any idea who ordered this?" asked Mikaela. The calm in her voice hid the intense anger she was feeling.

"Don't know, but I will find out. Right after I take care of a few things. Don't go home. You know what you need to do."

He was telling her to stay away from CATT and known places.

"I have a few calls to make and then I'm on my objective." said Mikaela.

"I would strongly advise against it, but who am I kidding?" he laughed, a short bark.

"Find that objective. He is tied to all of this somehow and it seems someone is very pissed," said David.

"How will I contact you?" said Mikaela.

"You won't. I'll contact you. Have my friend give you a phone and I will stay in touch. I have to go. Speak to you soon unless I'm dead of course." He hung up.

Chapter Thirty Eight

As John faced Lea, he knew that the other fights were merely preludes to this one. He took a deep breath and assessed Lea.

She was lean with a dancer's body, but John could see that she trained extensively in conditioning her body. Her knuckles were callused and John was willing to wager that everything that could be a weapon was just as conditioned.

They faced each other and bowed. John knew he would have to blur to a certain degree or this fight was over before it began. The question was how much before it became unfair? Lea answered the question for him. The sensation of pain blossomed in his solar plexus as air escaped his lungs and he dropped to one knee. Lea stood behind him. John winced as he caught his breath. John stood and turned to face Lea. He bowed slightly acknowledging the blow. She moved again and John blurred. Time seemed to stop. *She was fast* he admitted. He was faster.

As she prepared to strike, John grabbed her wrist and threw her. For a moment, she remained frozen in space then time snapped like a rubber band and she flew across the dojo floor, a look of surprise across her face. Twisting mid-air, she recovered and landed on her feet. John was impressed; few people could recover that well or that fast.

In an instant, she was upon him. She launched a barrage of hand strikes designed to distract him. The real threat came from the kick she threw in between the strikes. To the untrained, it would appear that she had only used her hands, her leg moved so fast the eye could not keep up with the technique. John was highly trained and saw the kick concealed in the feint. If he let it connect uncontrolled he'd wake up some time tomorrow, wondering what happened, it was too late to dodge so he opted to stop the kick and Lea.

He focused as he was taught, so many years ago. He needed to redirect the energy and his breath combining them with intention. He caught the kick on his left side and heard the bone break almost immediately. He had hardened his muscles but it wasn't enough to stop the force of the kick. They energy travelled through and fractured the first thing it encountered; in this case his ribs, two to be precise. He was definitely out of practice. He should have factored the force travelling through his body.

"Nice kick." said John through clenched teeth.

Lea stepped back into a relaxed fighting stance and looked at him.

"You may want to consider stopping now. I don't know how you're still standing but I'm certain you have a few broken ribs." said Lea.

John hated doing this without having the time but it couldn't be helped. He focused on the ribs and knitted them. He wasn't as elegant as Masami and it wasn't healing, but rather a technique his sensei had taught him to deal with breaks. The pain was intense and forced him to breathe shallow for a few moments. It was a stopgap measure and John didn't think he could take another kick there but for the moment he could continue.

"I'm a little out of practice. If you don't mind, I would like to continue," John said.

"Very well," Lea assumed a different fighting stance. She glided in on his left. Capitalize on the weakness. It's what he would have done. He shifted to his left, avoiding the elbow that would have smashed into his injured side. He blurred past her, touching her on the left shoulder and causing her deltoids to spasm. It rendered her arm useless. It didn't stop Lea. She launched herself at John, her arm hanging limp at her side. John stood waiting for her. He didn't want it to get out of hand. So far no permanent damage had been done. He wasn't sure it would remain that way if they continued. Before she could reach him, a hand shot out and grabbed her, holding her firm to the ground as if she had been nailed in place. The Sensei stood between Lea and John, his hand resting lightly on Lea's shoulder.

"I will speak with this man." said the Sensei in a low voice.

Lea bowed her head. "I apologize, Sensei."

"There is no need, the outcome was determined before the first blow."

John bowed to Lea.

"I believe my assistant can help with the injuries, Masami?" said John.

Masami walked over and placed a hand on Lea's shoulder, moments later Lea had full mobility in her arm.

"That was amazing. What did you do?" Lea said as she moved her arm tentatively.

"I think it's best if we speak to our guests privately." said the Sensei.

"Yes, yes of course." said Lea.

Turning to the class, Lea spoke to the students.

"Hajime, please continue!" Terrance began to lead the class in a series of drills as the Sensei stepped off the dojo floor into his private office followed by John, Masami and Lea.

Chapter Thirty Nine

This had proven to be a dead end. She was no closer to her objective. She needed to find another asset, someone higher up on the food chain. It needed to be someone who could provide her with some answers. She left the building and headed downtown, using her long coat to cover most of the blood. The Shadow Blades would not be so easily dismissed, had there been more she would have had considerable difficulty. *Analyze, assess, and adapt*, her instructor's voice came back to her.

She stopped at the next corner and took out her phone, punching in some numbers.

"Yes?" the voice was male.

"The information you gave me was a dead end. Shadow Blades were waiting for me." she said.

"Literally for them I'm guessing – Blades you say?" he asked.

"Yes, I need someone higher up. This is getting me nowhere."

"Not so, you now have the attention of the Blades which is no small matter. Do not underestimate their tenacity. They will not stop until you are a distant memory." said the voice.

She knew the Blades were relentless and if they were involved in this, she knew she was headed in the right direction.

"The name and a location," she said.

"Very well, the information is being sent to your phone. His name is Trevor, Trevor James, he will be at that location at that time. He should have some answers for you and if not… well, you can do what you do so well." the voice said.

She hung up the phone. Forty eight hours and she could have a clear path. She smiled.

Chapter Forty

Mikaela was angry. It wasn't the fact that someone wanted her dead and was framing her friend. She was accustomed to being disliked, hated even. It came with the job. What angered her was the subterfuge. She had always preferred a direct confrontation. You want to eliminate someone; you put a bullet between their eyes, a knife in their throat. This sending of lackeys to do your dirty work disgusted her. She sat quietly in the Rover, going through her options.

"What's the plan?" asked Helen.

"Look Helen –" started Mikaela.

"Stop, Don't even continue." said Helen.

"Things are going to get real messy real fast. You can still walk away," said Mikaela.

Helen looked at Mikaela for a moment before answering.

"David said you would try to lone wolf your way through this. I'm here to make sure you don't. I gave him my word." She turned to face Mikaela, then "My word is my bond. It's all I have. I do not give it lightly and once I do, I keep it."

"I understand," said Mikaela.

Helen hadn't realized she was gripping the steering wheel so tightly and eased up a bit. She blew out air forcefully to relieve some of her stress, an old nervous tic.

"So, what's the plan?" said Helen.

Mikaela looked out of the passenger side window. They had left George's place thirty minutes earlier and were headed downtown.

"Someone wants me erased, and it has to do with Kane. I don't respond well to threats Helen. They make me unreasonable. We need to regroup and plan a strategy. By then David should have contacted me." said Mikaela.

"And if he hasn't?"

"Then you and I are going to have to ask some questions in an unpleasant way." whispered Mikaela.

Helen smiled then.

"Let's go talk to John Kane." said Mikaela.

Chapter Forty One

John and Masami followed the Sensei into a private section of the school. The space was sparsely furnished with tatami mats covering the floor, a low wooden table in the center and several bookcases lining the walls. The Sensei sat before the table and gestured for John to sit before him. He looked at Lea.

"Tea, please Lea." said Himara.

Lea bowed and left the room. In the background, John could hear the class underway punctuated every so often by shouts. Masami sat behind John and to his right. No one spoke, each taking comfort in the blanket of silence that enveloped them. Lea entered with a tray and began serving tea. The set itself was a traditional Chado set and John noticed that she was quite skilled.

She served John and Masami as it was customary to serve guests first. Next she served the Sensei before retreating from the table. Throughout this process not a word was spoken. Once Lea was done, John sipped his tea.

"Exquisite." said John.

Lea bowed her head in acknowledgement.

"It is excellent." said the Sensei which was high praise indeed. Lea bowed again.

"I observed you have had some unique instruction." said the Sensei.

John knew this was his best chance at finding who was eliminating assets. If this Sensei did not teach them then he would know who did.

"Yes, Sensei my instruction was not what I would call common," said John.

The Sensei nodded.

"I was hoping you could help me Sensei." said John. He knew asking directly was risking the entire conversation. The Sensei's jaw tightened and John feared the worse then the saw the Sensei relax slightly.

"What do you wish to know?" said Himara.

John was unsure how to proceed. He decided to be frank and plain.

"Someone with very unique abilities has been eliminating certain individuals. These abilities are unique enough that there could be at most two or three Sensei with the skill to impart such knowledge in this entire city. I need to find this person before more death occurs." said John.

John knew that at most it could only be three people. The Sensei sitting before him was one, the person who had taught the assassin, and himself.

"If I give you this person's name, what will you do with this information?" asked Himara.

"I will need to have a conversation with the Sensei in question." said John.

"A conversation? You may not like where that conversation leads." said Sensei Himara.

"Father, you can't!" exclaimed Lea from his side. He raised his hand to silence her.

"We must or we will be as responsible." said Himara.

Lea remained silent.

"Please forgive my daughter. She is still young and impetuous."

Lea's cheeks reddened as she kept her face down.

"No apologies are necessary, Sensei," said John as he stole a glance at Lea. He didn't want to cause her any more shame.

"Are you prepared to follow this course of action to its end?" said the Sensei.

"I am," said John.

The Sensei nodded and drank some tea.

"The man you are looking for goes by the name of Shinichi."

John held his breath as the bottom fell out from his world. Masami let out a breath.

"Are you certain?" asked John.

The Sensei nodded and drank some more tea.

Shinichi was the name used by Satoshi Fujita Nakamura, John's deceased teacher.

Chapter Forty Two

Mikaela pulled out her laptop. She had learned long ago never to leave it at any site. They had parked in Dumbo, near the Brooklyn Bridge in order to be able to access the other boroughs easily. She loaded the program that tracked John's laptop and expected to find that the signal had vanished. Surprised, she found that the signal was still active.

"Let's go!" she said to Helen.

"Where to?" said Helen as she turned on the Rover.

"Williamsburg to be precise." She gave Helen the closest address to the signal.

"That's in the middle of nowhere according to the GPS." said Helen.

"That's where we're going. Let's find out what's in the middle of nowhere while we still have a signal." said Mikaela.

"You realize it could be a diversion, gets us all the way in Brooklyn and he isn't even there." said Helen.

Mikaela agreed but the signal had not moved from its location in a few hours.

"It's the best lead we have. We may as well follow it." said Mikaela.

She really hoped the signal led to John Kane. She had a few questions to ask him.

Chapter Forty Three

"We have found them, Sir," the Blade spoke into the phone quietly, almost a whisper.

"Please explain to me why we are discussing this while they are still alive?" Kage said calmly.

"There is a – complication."

"Elaborate."

"The targets entered a building which appears to be a school of some sort."

"And this is a complication how?" said Kage.

Kage's patience was beginning to erode.

"No Sir, that isn't the complication. As we secured the vehicle, we realized it was emitting a signal. At first we thought it was the vehicle itself but it is a computer within the vehicle."

It was standard procedure for the Blades to sweep for tracking devices when encountering unknown vehicles or locations. Kage had begun the procedure and it had saved him needless losses of men as well as kept his locations secret.

Kage pondered this for a moment. It was certainly an unforeseen factor. Who was tracking his target? It would be imprudent to discount this person.

"Secure the vehicle, eliminate everyone in the school. When the person tracking the signal arrives, bring him to me – alive."

"Yes Sir."

"Do you have enough men to accomplish this?"

"Yes Sir, four Hands." answered the Blade.

A hand consisted of five Blades.

"Good leave a Hand to secure the vehicle, the rest go to the school, no one leaves." said Kage.

"Yes Sir," the Blade hung up and began giving instructions to the other group leaders. Silently they made their way to the dojo of Sensei Fujita Himara.

Chapter Forty Four

Kei woke up sore. Her training had been short of outright torture but only just. She had to admit she was getting better. The broth and tea did work miracles. Maybe she could stay at this dojo and finish her training. Before she came and made her leave, again.

Each time she found a dojo with a decent Sensei, it wasn't long before she showed up and made her leave. Maybe this time, if she saw that she was really training hard, maybe she could stay. The family journal looked like it could be helpful in getting through her training. She read a few more pages before she had to get out of bed. The description of training in those pages made what she was going through sound like a vacation. She heard the class in the dojo.

"They must have gotten a late start." She thought to herself. It wasn't unusual. Sometimes the Sensei would demonstrate a technique he wanted them to work on. She looked at the clock on her dresser. Eight am was late even if the Sensei had been giving one of the demos.

She got dressed quickly and started toward the dojo. As she walked by the large window in the corridor that joined the sleeping quarters with the main area, she saw them. A group of men approached the school. When they arrived at the entrance, they each drew short swords with black blades. Fear coursed through her like an electric jolt. She started running.

The Blades made their way up the stairs to the dojo. Single file, they stepped quietly until they were almost up the dojo proper. The lead blade entered the reception area followed by two more Blades.

"May I help –" she never had a chance to finish her sentence; the lead Blade pulled the dagger from her neck and wiped the blood off.

"There is a class in session. Remove any witnesses," he said pointing to a group of five.

"You search the living quarters," he said pointing to another group. We will find the targets."

Each group headed off in a different direction.

"How can that be? My Sensei is deceased." said John.

He could barely form the words.

"Did you see him die?" asked the Sensei.

"No, but my source was trusted and reliable." John said, thinking back to Trevor; wondering how trusted he really was.

At one point, he would have trusted Trevor with his life, but that was many years ago. Times and people change.

"It is possible I have been led to believe my Sensei was deceased. I do not know the reason yet, but I will find out." said John.

"That will have to wait. We have more pressing matters. Intruders have entered the school, no doubt seeking you." said the Sensei.

"How many?" said John.

"I can sense fifteen in groups of five." said Himara.

John was surprised, he had never been able to sense more than two or three and his Sensei, five at most.

"Where are they." said John.

John was on his feet, Masami beside him.

"They are splitting up, dojo, living areas and here." said Himara.

Masami knew what they were.

"Groups of five, Sensei?" she asked.

He paused a moment then nodded.

"You know these men?" said Himara.

"Yes, these are men of the Kage, Shadow Blades." said Masami.

Kei ran down the hall and almost ran into the group of Blades headed towards the living quarters, as she turned a corner.

"Whoa," she said as she skidded to a stop several feet away.

She drew her short sword. Lea had taught her to never go without a weapon. For indoor, close quarters fighting she preferred her short sword, longer than a knife and in her hands, just as versatile.

The five Blades drew their swords. The size of the corridor forced them to stand shoulder to shoulder.

"I will handle her. Step back." said the lead.

Dressed in what appeared to be black military gear, the leader stepped forward to meet Kei.

"So what are you guys like, ninja?" asked Kei. She couldn't resist; all they needed were the masks and the outfit would be complete. She began to slowly step back.

"Not quite, what we are would give ninjas nightmares," said the lead Blade.

"I see, so I'm guessing this is not going to be an instructional sparring session?" said Kei.

"You talk too much little girl," he said then lunged.

Kei had been using the banter to distance herself from the group, effectively drawing the leader back towards her. The ploy had worked, somewhat. The group of four was further away, not as far as she would have liked, but it would have to do.

As he lunged, she twisted to the right, allowing the lunge to continue past her. It was amateurish at best and it pissed her off that he thought that little of her skills to attack this way. She clamped down on her anger and slit his throat. The Kevlar material around his neck was no match for her sword, which sliced through it with ease.

"Please tell me he wasn't the best of your group. I mean, really?" she said.

She pushed his body with her foot into the center of the corridor, never taking her eyes off the remaining four Blades. They started approaching. She set herself in a fighting stance designed to maximize the limited space then turned and ran.

Lea made it to the dojo in time to see Erica die. Erica had shaken off her fight with John and was on the dojo floor near the entrance working on some techniques when the first Blade entered. She never had a chance. The blade entered silently and ran his sword through her from behind. Lea entering the dojo from the opposite end could see the surprise and pain etched on Erica's face as she collapsed to the floor.

131

"Everyone out now!" shouted Lea.

Everyone quickly began filing out. Terrance wanted to remain but Lea pushed him on.

"Go with them and keep them safe. I will deal with these cowards." said Lea.

"You sure?" said Terrence.

His voice had choked up, his words tight with emotion. Erica had been a fellow student, and more importantly a good friend.

"I am absolutely certain." she said as she walked over to a weapons rack and drew two swords.

Four more Blades had entered the dojo as Terrance ushered out the remaining students and locked the door behind him. The Blade leader bent down and calmly wiped his sword on Erica's body. Then he turned and faced Lea.

"You only delay the inevitable. We will find them and kill them all." he slowly stood as he said this.

"I'm going to kill you last. I want you to understand how inevitable your death will be. I will however show you the same courtesy you showed my friend. I will make it swift," said Lea.

"We will wait here." said Himara.

Everyone remained seated. John and Masami looked at each other. His voice entertained no argument. He sipped his tea. As he placed his cup down, the Blades entered the room silently.

"Please." the Sensei beckoned to the lead Blade, "if you would indulge an old man who is about to die, why are you here?"

The Blade looked around at the others who nodded.

"We are here for them." he said as he pointed to John and Masami.

"The Kage leaves no witnesses."

The implication was clear. The Sensei put his cup down slowly.

"I understand now, very well. Are you certain I cannot dissuade you from this course of action?"

All the Blades drew their swords.

"I will take that as a no." said Himara.

The Sensei stood and signaled to John and Masami to not interfere. He stood to face the Blades. They had fanned out to prevent any escape with the lead flanked by two Blades on each side. Himara, who was dressed in a loose fitting gi with hakama, looked unassuming as the Blades began to advance. Even though John knew Himara was highly skilled, he was also quite old. Masami as if reading his thoughts pulled him back to the wall to prevent him from interfering.

The lead Blade turned to John and spoke.

"You would let an old man –" he pointed his swords at Himara as he said this, "die in your place. Where is your honor?"

It was a calculated ploy to goad John into a rash action. On some level it worked, John could feel his ears warming up, but he didn't let any emotion show on his face.

"Death is not always the alternative," said Himara. "A pointless death is just a waste of life."

"You are no threat to us old man. Kill him." the lead Blade said. Two Blades approached the Sensei. John could sense the subtle change come over Himara. The time for talk was over. It was now time to act, to kill. John almost felt sorry for the Blades, until he remembered that they were here to kill him and Masami. John turned to Masami.

"These Blades are not like the other group." he said.

"The Shadow Blades have several groups. The rank and file is sent to attack secondary targets, causing the enemy to spread themselves thin. The elite groups are sent after the real targets." said Masami.

This group was meant to face the highest possible threat. John could see it in their stances and approach. The second two Blades slowly started to approach Himara with the lead holding back. John had never seen anyone move so fast, outside of blurring. Himara evaded the first cut which would have slit his throat by a fraction of an inch. Immediately ducking and stepping to the side avoided two more attacks. Pivoting on his back foot put him out of reach of the fourth attack which would have sliced open his thigh.

"He can't dodge them forever, why doesn't he attack?" said John to Masami. She placed a hand on his arm to calm him and to subtly remind him not to intervene.

His skill is so great that it's possible he could dodge them for quite some time, thought John. That wouldn't resolve this situation though.

"He is not dodging, he is observing. Watch him closely," said Masami.

John focused on Himara and noticed every time he dodged an attack, he would scan his entire opponent, something that seemed odd to John.

"Why is he doing that," asked John, without taking his eyes off Himara.

"Because of his skill, it is the first step in defeating an opponent, know your enemy," said Masami.

John really had to make the time to read the journal given to him by Fujita Sensei. He had a feeling it would explain these skills. John was transfixed. It was akin to watching someone jump into a blender and exit unscathed.

The first Blade fell, blood oozing from his mouth and nose. He fell suddenly clutching his throat, in a few moments he was still.

"What was that? What happened?" said John.

Masami was silent for a moment until John turned to her. He could see the fear in her eyes.

"What's wrong? What is it?" asked John.

After what seemed an eternity, Masami exhaled.

"He knows more than two of the skills." she whispered. "No one outside the clan heads is supposed to acquire that knowledge. It is forbidden."

John knew the implications. *Was this the person he was looking for? Was he lying about his Sensei being alive? If he needed to, could he defeat him?*

Those questions would have to wait. John saw Himara appear to brush his hand across the chest of one of the blades as he sidestepped a vertical cut. It almost seemed as if Himara were steadying himself to present a fall. A moment later, the Blade fell to the ground, gasping for breath.

"He stopped his lungs." said Masami.

The other two Blades though wary, were undeterred and attacked in unison.

Himara managed to dodge one Blade stepping slightly to the right. Touching the Blades hand as he stepped, he caused him to drop his sword as his hand immediately cramped forcing his fingers into a claw. The second Blade was much faster than he anticipated and managed to cut Himara across the abdomen, eliciting a grunt from the old man. Himara drew close to the Blade catching his wrist with one hand and driving a finger into his temple with the other. The blade was dead before he hit the ground.

"Impressive." said the lead Blade as he surveyed the three dead Blades.

"It seems you forgot one." he said as he walked over to the Blade clutching his hand in agony as his fingers were being forced apart by his very body.

"Let me ease your pain." the lead Blade said as he bent down to survey the hand that was now so contorted, the bones had begun snapping.

"Rest easy brother." he said as he slit the Blade's throat.

The lead blade turned to the Sensei as he spoke.

"You hid yourself well. Had the Kage known of your existence, we would have been here earlier." said the lead Blade.

Himara Sensei looked over at John. In that second, no words were necessary. John knew the sensei was done.

"This one is yours." said Himara as he collapsed. Masami rushed to the Sensei as John stepped to intercept the lead Blade.

"It is a futile gesture, your death is as inevitable as the old mans." The Blade turned to face John.

"I'm not dead yet." said John.

"We will see."

The Blade took a defensive position. John could hear the Sensei whisper something to Masami as she bent close.

"Masami," John called over his shoulder, "what did he say?"

"Poison, the swords are covered in poison!" said Masami.

The lead Blade smiled as he looked at John.

"Now at the end, you finally understand." the Blade said as he stepped forward.

Kei hoped they would follow her. She was leading them away from the living quarters and towards the dojo.

136

She made a right down the corridor that led to the dojo looking back to make sure they were behind her. The glass doors at the end of the corridor offered her an unobstructed view of the dojo floor. She saw Lea and more men in the dojo. She looked at Lea saw death on her face. Kei turned to face the Blades chasing her.

"Guess it will have to be here then." she said to herself.

If she was going to die, she couldn't think of a better way to do it. She could only hope for a death that would make her Sensei proud.

She held her blade in an inverse grip designed to fool her opponent into thinking no attack was possible. The first Blade came at her with a horizontal slash designed to disembowel. She stepped in at the end of his arc and stabbed through his heart. She had no illusions about her skill; she was good but not that good.

These guys aren't even second string? she thought. Too late she realized the sacrifice tactic. With her Blade buried in the Blade's chest, a second Blade came up behind the first and stabbed through him. She wasn't run through because they wielded short swords. The sword penetrated her right side, and she drew back in pain.

"Shit, that move was just low." she said.

She blurred, anger and fear fueling her. She punched the Blade that stabbed her in the throat, killing him, while deflecting another strike from the third Blade. Pulling a knife from her thigh sheath, she turned 180 degrees driving it into his neck burying it to the hilt. That's when the floor began to tilt and she stumbled back.

"You bitches use poison? What the hell?" she said as she steadied herself against the wall.

The fourth Blade seeing the opportunity jumped at her, slicing upwards. She deflected the blow just barely and blurred placing her hand on his chest. Or at least that was her plan. The poison had thrown off her timing so instead of his chest, she stumbled and grabbed his arm instead. She destroyed the muscles in his arm, rendering it useless. He dropped his sword and was about to attack when she ran her sword through his abdomen several times.

She fell to the floor, her vision cloudy. She crawled to the dojo door and sat roughly against the wall, it was really more of a controlled fall. She used her foot and managed to get the door open, she had to warn Lea.

"Lea, their swords are covered in poison!" she yelled.

Her speech was beginning to slur and the floor began to sway under her. Lea didn't appear to acknowledge her, but she was certain she heard. She was tired all of a sudden. It seemed like a great moment to rest, to just sit here and catch her breath. She put her head back and closed her eyes.

Lea heard Kei and filed the information away – *Don't get cut.* She saw Kei fall, saw the blood and realized she would probably be dead soon. She filed that as well – *kill them fast, help Kei.* She advanced on the Blades and blurred.

The first Blade came at her, a diagonal strike designed to cut from clavicle to abdomen. She parried and sliced horizontally behind her, catching the Blade there by surprise and spilling his intestines. Continuing the circle but descending, she removed the second attacker's leg at the thigh. As he fell, she removed his head. She immediately ducked under a slash at her head and removed the arm of the third Blade. As the fourth Blade lunged, she parried the thrust and using her second blade, slit his throat.

The lead Blade looked nervous but stepped forward. Lea ran towards him, blades trailing behind her, at the last second before what appeared to be impact; she slid to the left and sliced through the lead Blade. He fell slowly to the floor, his torso separated from his legs.

"What is the antidote?" she asked him.

She didn't dare get closer than arm's length because his nails or even saliva could contain the poison.

"I can make this death swift or leave you here to die, slowly. It's up to you," she said impassively.

With a blood stained finger, he drew a character on the floor then looked at her pleadingly.

With one last stroke, she ended his pain and his life. She ran to where Kei was, hoping she had the antidote in reach.

John wanted to ask why, but knew it was pointless. This was a foot soldier not a general. He took orders, carried them out and didn't ask questions. No, John would have to find the one responsible for giving the orders, when they met, and they would, John would ask him why. For now he had to survive this fight.

John, unlike the Sensei, did not possess the ability to dodge indefinitely. He held a short sword, grabbed from one of the dead Blades. If there was poison on it, he couldn't see it. The sword was light in his hand; he preferred a katana or even his gun but had neither at hand, so this would have to do.

"I promise you a swift death, if you surrender now. I think it's the most honorable thing you could do," said the lead Blade.

John didn't respond. Instead he swung the short sword several times getting a feel for its heft.

"I can't promise you the same," said John as he stepped closer to his opponent.

Most fights are ugly, inelegant affairs. John learned this truth early on in his training. The other thing he learned is most violent encounters only last several seconds to a few minutes at most. It's not a very long time, strictly speaking, unless of course you are on the receiving end of the violence. Then it seems to take forever as time stretches out, pulls up a chair and lounges, watching you fight for your life.

When a fight involved weapons, the ugly and inelegant parts are usually accompanied by copious amounts of bodily fluids, primarily blood. John couldn't take a chance and get cut even if Masami could heal him. He doubted he would be around long enough to receive the healing.

Without warning, the lead Blade blurred to John's right side, slashing at his arm. Only his training saved him as he managed to get his sword up in time to deflect the slash. John realized his disadvantage, the lead Blade only needed to cut him deep enough for the toxin on his sword to enter John's bloodstream. John however did not have that luxury, he was sure they would be immune or at least resistant to the poison used on their blades. The fact that the Blade could blur only reinforced the idea that someone was training people in this skill. This complicated matters only because John wanted answers and it was impossible to get answers from corpses.

It meant John couldn't kill this Blade, at least not immediately and this would shape how he would have to fight. Even though the Blade could blur, he wasn't proficient at it. Like a child learning to walk, he was uncertain and unbalanced. John could use that to his advantage. The Blade stepped back after his initial strike. John could see the surprise in his eyes; he didn't expect to have to use more than one strike.

"Where did you learn to do that?" asked John. "It's quite impressive."

The Blade only grunted. John knew he was feeling the effects of the blur. Until you trained extensively,

140

blurring was the equivalent of a hundred yard dash in a half a second, with the same effects.

"Right now I'm guessing you're feeling a bit winded maybe even dizzy. Your heart is racing and in a few moments your body will catch up with what you just did and heat up." said John.

The Blade wiped a hand across his brow.

"This will cause you to sweat, a lot."

John remembered the feelings well, the exhaustion, the relentless training to condition his body. It took him close to ten years before he could blur without the side effects being too pronounced.

John blurred. Fast enough to strike and shatter bone, not fast enough to kill in one blow. Using the pommel of his sword, he shattered the Blade's right collarbone, rendering the arm useless. The Blade took a step back with a sharp intake of breath being the only indicator he was feeling pain. Not even a grimace crossed his face. The Blade switched the sword to his left hand. John understood it must have been their training that allowed them to deal with the pain.

"Who trained you?" asked John.

"Why is that relevant? It will not change the outcome," said the Blade.

"I would like to know who taught you the ability you are wielding so poorly," said John.

The Blade narrowed his eyes.

"In addition, he sent you out before you were ready. It's like giving a three year old a gun. More likely to shoot itself than anyone else, if he even knows how to pull the trigger," said John.

The Blade blurred to John's left. John expected the move, even as he knew it would fail. It was a blurring slash designed to cut while in motion. A devastating attack if it connected. John shifted away and brought his hand down on the Blade's forearm shattering bone in the process. The Blade dropped his sword, pain etched on his face. Apparently he had reached his pain threshold.

"One more time, who trained you?" said John.

"I will die with my honor intact," he said as he bit the inside of his cheek, releasing a neurotoxin that immediately shut down his respiratory system, forcing him to fall back and suffocate.

"What a twisted sense of honor." said John as the Blade died on the floor. John walked over to Masami and Himara after making sure the Blade was dead.

"How is he?" said John.

The Sensei's wound was looking better, but he was still pale.

"He will live, but it will be sometime before he will be whole. Only his training saved him." said Masami.

Himara Sensei opened his eyes, his breathing still ragged.

"My training and your skill, you were not supposed to save an old man. Why did you do it?" said Himara.

"What is he talking about, what does he mean?" said John.

Masami was about to answer when Lea came running in.

"I need your help, now." she said pointing at Masami as she ran off. Himara nodded and Masami stood and ran after her.

Chapter Forty Five

"What did you mean; she wasn't supposed to save you? Why not?" said John.

Himara opened his eyes briefly before answering.

"It is our way," he said slowly, each word an effort.

"Knowing one skill makes one formidable; learning more than one is prohibited and is a death sentence.

Outside of clan heads there are no exceptions to this; it is the way it has been since the beginning." said Himara.

John could understand the logic, and it was similar to what Jiro Sensei had alluded to. He didn't know about the death sentence.

"Does this put Masami in danger, if she helped you and wasn't supposed to?" said John.

"She will be in danger only if we alert the proper authorities regarding this. Which as I see it, don't need to be informed about such a trivial matter."

John agreed.

"If this one ability rule has always been in place, how did you learn more than one?" said John.

"My Sensei did not believe in this rule as you call it. He believed it made us weak and fractured the clan. He wasn't the only one who felt this way and so secretly he arranged for me to receive instruction from another Sensei. He swore me to secrecy and I knew my life was forfeit if I ever revealed my other abilities." said Himara.

"When the rules chafe, they are usually broken." said John.

The Sensei nodded.

"I wanted to speak to you because someone is using an ability to murder others." said John.

"And you thought I may have taught this person, I understand. You did not expect to hear your Sensei's name as a possibility and yet it is possible." said Himara.

John nodded.

"It is possible the young woman we have here may be of some assistance. Her name is Kei." said Himara.

"Where is this Kei?" said John.

"She is usually in the living quarters but with this attack, I'm certain she is fighting somewhere." said the Sensei as he grew pensive.

"I need to speak to her." said John.

"My daughter would know her exact location."

John nodded and stood up to find Lea.

" Will you be OK?" said John.

"I'm old and tired but I still have a few years ahead of me. Go." he said, waving his hand. "Find Lea and she will assist you. I will be fine."

John propped up the Sensei making him as comfortable as possible.

"I'll be back soon." said John.

"I will be right here." said Himara.

John left the room and headed towards the living quarters. The Sensei didn't tell him that Masami couldn't stop the spread of the poison long term; all she could do was delay the inevitable. He had lost too much blood. He had lived a full life and had few, if any, regrets. Moving over to the table where he kept writing materials, he began to write a letter. After a few minutes, he folded and addressed it. He slowly sat back and leaned against a wall. He could feel the toxin in his system.

After catching his breath, he went over to his resting area and lay down and closed his eyes for the last time.

John found Lea in the hallway that connected the living quarters to the dojo proper. Kei was on the floor with Masami over her. He looked at Lea who slowly shook her head.

"Masami is she -?" said John.

"Not dead, no, but it doesn't look good. This toxin is something I have never encountered. It is difficult to fight. Usually if I'm familiar with a toxin, it makes it easier to deal with and stop." said Masami.

Her brow glistened with sweat and John could see the strain on her face. He walked a little closer to Lea.

"Is that Kei?" he asked.

Lea nodded. "She was very skilled but she was cut."

She let the words hang in the air. John knew the rest; Kei slowly came around and began stirring. For a moment, her gaze was unfocused and then she recognized Lea. She looked at the faces and knew it was bad.

"How long?" she asked.

Masami hung her head.

"I'm sorry the poison is just too strong." said Masami.

Tears flowed down Masami's face.

Kei asked again softly. "How long, how long do I have?"

"Maybe an hour, before your body shuts down – I'm sorry," said Masami.

Kei's eyes began to water.

"This isn't exactly how I pictured my life ending, but I guess sometimes we don't get to choose huh?"

John walked over to where Kei sat on the floor now.

"My name is John, I'm really sorry about this. Is there anything I can do for you?"

"Give me a few more years?" Kei half joked as she fought back tears of her own.

The look on John's face answered her question. She turned away to hide her face.

"No, I guess not," Kei said as she laughed bitterly. She turned to John then, an intensity igniting her eyes.

"Yeah, there is something you can do for me, John is it?"

John nodded not trusting his voice to speak.

"You find out who sent them and you kill him. Can you do that for me?" said Kei.

"I promise on my life. I will make sure those responsible pay for this." said John.

Kei smiled then, a sad smile. "Thank you."

John could see that she was getting weaker.

145

"Can I ask you one more thing?" John said as he sat beside her.

'Yeah, sure, it's not like I'm going anywhere." said Kei.

"Lea tells me you are very skilled – that you can blur. Is that true?"

"Guess I wasn't skilled enough. Yes I can blur - funny that's what my Sensei called it too."

"Can you tell me his name?" asked John.

"I never said him - that's so typical." said Kei.

"I apologize; it's just that it is a very rare skill. I was not aware any female Sensei had this skill," said John.

"It's ok," said Kei as she began to cough. The coughing lasted about thirty seconds before she was able to regain her breath.

"Can you tell me her name?" said John.

"Sure as far as I know she was the only Sensei who knew the ability. She told me her Sensei had been killed. Her name, my Sensei's name is Rukio."

How could Rukio still be alive? John needed to make sure.

"Are you certain?" asked John.

"Yes, I'm certain. Are you kidding me, really?" said Kei.

"I'm sorry Kei. It's just that I knew a Rukio long ago but she was killed." said John still in disbelief.

"Yeah I'm sorry too. Can I speak to Lea a moment?" said Kei.

"Of course." said John.

John beckoned to Lea, who was speaking quietly with Masami. Lea came right over and held Kei's hand.

"I'm so sorry Kei." she said as she caressed Kei's forehead.

Lea could feel Kei was burning up. Her body was trying to fight the poison and losing. Kei looked at Lea.

146

"Thank you, thank you for everything." said Kei.

Lea shushed her. "It was my honor," said Lea. John left her side and joined Masami. He didn't want to intrude on what felt like an intimate moment. Besides he was still shell shocked as he shared with Masami what Kei had told him.

"I saw her die, Masami." said John.

"You saw an explosion and assumed she died in it. That is not the same thing." said Masami quietly.

John remained silent. He knew she was right. The bigger question lay before him. *Why fake her death, what purpose did it serve? Whose purpose did it serve?*

Lea silently joined John and Masami.

"She's gone." said Lea.

John and Masami remained silent.

"She was a good fighter, a strong warrior. That is how we will remember her." said Lea.

John nodded as he went over to where Kei lay. He picked up her body and walked to the dojo. John caught Terrence's eyes and shook his head. Terrence pointed to a corner of the dojo where they were putting the bodies of the deceased.

John walked over to the far corner of the dojo and gently placed Kei on the floor. He was given a sheet to cover her body. As he did so, he looked around the dojo. John realized that if he didn't end this, more people would die. He had to find Rukio; she had the answers he needed.

Mikaela walked up to the car. The earpiece in her left ear chirped to life.

"I have eyes on you." said Helen. "Perimeter is clear."

Mikaela didn't like the idea of being bait, since the bait usually ended up dead. This was only marginally more acceptable because Helen had a Barrett M107 and was focused on her position. She knew that eventually someone would show up at the car.

"I've got movement. Check your six." said Helen.

Mikaela turned just in time to see Helen transform the head of the Blade into a red mist. The round was so powerful it continued through the Blade and punched a hole in the car. She saw the short sword in his hand and realized his intent.

"Any more, do you see any more?" said Mikaela.

"Yes you need to move. Come to me. I'll cover you." said Helen. Mikaela looked down the street and saw more figures headed her way.

"Remember to leave one alive." said Mikaela.

"I'll do my best. You need to move now before I have to take them all out. Stay in my line of sight." said Helen.

The figures were getting closer, Mikaela could count four of them, and each had swords drawn. Mikaela began to run. She had to run in a straight line to draw her pursuers after her.

The fact that Helen had eliminated one so close to her only led to the illusion that she was alone. It looked as if Mikaela had shot him at point blank range. That illusion wouldn't last very long once Helen got started. As if on cue, Helen took out the last Blade in the group chasing Mikaela. She eliminated them in sequence until one Blade remained.

"You're going to have to take him down. If I do it there won't be much left to ask questions of." said Helen.

"Can't you hit a leg or arm or something?" said Mikaela as she ran.

"I could –" said Helen drawing out the word. "You do realize this is a Barrett M107? Anything I hit will result in the disintegration of said target. And I mean that quite literally." said Helen.

"Shit, fine." Mikaela said under her breath as she turned around. She drew her Glock immediately and stopped running.

"Here are your choices; you can die now in a spectacular fashion as my partner erases you like she did your friends." said Mikaela.

The Blade, expecting the others to catch up to him turned his head quickly and realized he was alone. He dropped his sword.

"Or you can answer my questions and I give you my word you will walk away. If not I can put a bullet through you and call it a day. What's it going to be?" Mikaela held the Glock to the Blades' forehead.

The Blade looked at her a moment, thinking.

"What questions?" he said after a few moments of silence.

"Smart man, why are you here?" said Mikaela.

She didn't lower her gun as she asked the questions, staying alert to any movement on his part.

"Our job was to secure the vehicle. That's all I know." he said.

The Blade sounded young, maybe mid-twenties, his voice cracked as he answered.

"Who sent you?" Mikaela knew she couldn't let him live, but she would try and get as much information as she could.

"The Kage always sends us."

Who the hell was the Kage? Mikaela was about to ask her next question when the Blade's head disappeared, along with the upper part of his torso.

"Helen! What the hell!" yelled Mikaela.

"It wasn't me! Get down!" Mikaela dove for cover as Helen scanned the area.

"Anything?" asked Mikaela.

"Gimme a sec I'm looking." said Helen.

There were too many vantage points to search them all from her position.

"It seems they only wanted to silence him. Make yourself scarce, I'll meet you back at the car. Be careful heading back." said Helen. Mikaela replayed the image again in her mind. It was possible there wasn't another sniper hiding in the shadows. This looked like a very controlled explosion. Was it possible they were wired to explode and didn't know it? She headed back to the car. The more she thought of it, the more sense it made.

"I think he was wired and someone detonated him." Mikaela said to Helen as she wiped the blood and gore from her face.

"That's some retirement plan." said Helen.

"Tell me about it but it explains a lot. Stay up there and keep your eyes on the car. I'm going to make sure our friend John doesn't drive away." said Mikaela.

Mikaela ran back to the car and shot two of the tires. The silenced Glock sounded like a whisper as it ejected bullets into the tires. Mikaela observed the tires, expecting them to go flat. They remained intact.

"What gives?" asked Helen. "Is he using run flats?"

Mikaela looked at the tire and saw that her bullets had penetrated but caused no damage.

"I have never seen this before in my life, outside a Bond movie." said Mikaela.

"That's probably where they got the idea from," said a voice behind her. She whirled around seeing a figure in the shadows. "Tell your friend to come down or she gets to watch you die," said the voice.

"I heard, be there in three minutes," said Helen.

"She'll be here in three minutes." said Mikaela.

150

"In the meantime why not introduce ourselves - you are Mikaela Petrovich, probably the most effective person at CATT."

Mikaela glared. "And who are you?" she said.

"Me? I represent a group with a vested interest in the outcome of John's arrival here. My name is Trevor. We can all wait for John to arrive. I'm sure he will be here shortly." said Trevor as he stepped forward pointing a gun at Mikaela.

Chapter Forty Six

John's cell phone vibrated in his pocket and he opened it. It was Mole.

"John? John?" said Mole.

"Yes, what is it Mole?"

"Still alive - That's good man. It's getting crazy down there."

"You have no idea." said John.

"Actually I do but that's another convo. Something rocked the car pretty hard. You may want to go check it." said Mole.

"Got it, I'm on my way." Masami looked at John.

"Something is wrong with the car. I'm going to check it out." Masami stood to go when John stopped her.

"Where are you going?" said John.

"What do you mean where am I going. We are going to the car." said Masami.

It wasn't a request. John knew how to pick his battles and this one was lost before he even started.

"'John?" Mole was still on the phone.

"Yeah, I'm going to the car now." said John.

"Yeah about that – whatever hit the car, hit it with enough firepower to rock a tank. Just thought you should know. You know as in dangerous?" said Mole.

"Got it, lots of firepower, sounds like a certain person I know has caught up." said John.

"Ice queen?"

"I'll let you know." said John.

With that John hung up. He knew there were quite a few weapons that could pack that kind of firepower. He wasn't going to take any chances. Together with Masami, he walked several blocks out of the way and climbed to the roof of an adjacent building to look down at the car. He got to the roof of a building a few blocks away with an unobstructed view.

He saw Mikaela, some other woman and Trevor. *What the hell was Trevor doing here? Was he working with Mikaela now? And who was the other woman?* She looked ex-military, seriously ex-military. Trevor was looking up at the rooftops surrounding him.

"If I were John, would I come straight to the car, I think not. What do you think ladies?" said Trevor.

"I think that if he's smart, he puts a bullet between your eyes and ends you." said Helen.

Trevor laughed.

"No, no that's not John's style. He's more of the up close and snuff you out kind of guy."

"Pity." whispered Helen.

'John! I know you can hear me!" yelled Trevor.

"I guess he needs some motivation." said Trevor to himself. Trevor pointed the gun at Helen's chest and fired. At such proximity, the force of the shot sent her over the hood of the car to land on the other side, a look of surprise on her face.

"It is a trap." said Masami quietly.

"Come on down John, or she's next!" Trevor pointed the gun at Mikaela.

John stood up. "Stay here." he told Masami.

"Ah there you are, come on John, let's talk."

"Don't hurt her Trevor." Ten minutes later John was at street level.

"That hero complex will get you killed one day John." said Trevor.

"Trevor, what the hell are you doing? You called me remember?" said John.

"I know, I know, but it seems my superiors are getting impatient John. You remember what I told you about not producing?" said Trevor.

"That they would start looking at me." said John.

"Exactly, where do you think they are looking now, John?"

"I can guess." said John.

"Now now, in case you're thinking of doing your thing, I wouldn't. The moment I sense any movement from you, even a slight breeze, I pull this trigger and end her. We both know you aren't that fast." said Trevor.

John stood still.

"This was never about the assets, was it?" said John.

"Oh no, I'm sure someone is concerned about the loss of assets. It just isn't me." said Trevor.

"This was a retirement op?" said John.

Retirement ops were undertaken to remove potential or perceived threats. On occasion they were used internally to remove assets that had become dangerous or no longer useful.

"Something like that, John. I'm sorry it came to this but apparently someone doesn't want you around anymore."

"Trevor, this is a bad idea." said John slowly.

"You know John, initially I thought so. Then I thought, with you out of the way and unrestricted access to CATT. Well, not so bad an idea."

"Why CATT, What does CATT have to do with this?" said Mikaela.

153

"You want to do the honors, John?" said Trevor.

"Access, by now he has disrupted the hierarchy of the organization, primed to place one of his people to run it. This means you are in the way, a loose end." said John.

"Exactly and I am not known to be sloppy. Don't worry Mrs. Petrovich; there are a few people interested in your talents. I don't think they will kill you, at least not until you've outlived your usefulness." said Trevor.

"David - no." said Mikaela.

"Oh I'm afraid the position for the director of CATT will be vacant very soon, probably even as we speak. Placing kill orders on you and your boss was quite the challenge. However once it was in, well they jumped right to it. It was as if they didn't like you Mrs. Petrovich." said Trevor.

Trevor favored chest shots. It was the years of training and his particular method of execution. John remembered asking him about it once.

"Headshots are too immediate, no pain. I like to see the life leave their eyes." was his response. John counted on this.

"Keys and code please and don't lie to me John. I would hate to have to shoot it out of her." said Trevor.

John tossed the car keys and told him the code.

"Thank you. Now we have to conclude this conversation. If you blur, the second bullet goes into her and she, unlike you cannot blur. Are you ready?" asked Trevor.

John nodded. Trevor fired.

Chapter Forty Seven

"What's our situation, Rogers?" said David.

"Sir, we are down two squads. They just keep throwing men at the problem."

"I'm going to assume that problem is us, Rogers." said David.

"Yes Sir." said Rogers.

"Someone with a lot of weight and very connected friends wants us to go away."

"It would appear so, Sir."

"Well, Rogers, I'm nothing if not accommodating. Get the explosives. Switch frequencies and let them hear us. Give them our location and let them pinpoint us." said David.

"Sir?" asked Rogers.

"Yes, that will give away our position. Tell the men to fall back before we suffer any more casualties. Make sure to lure them here." said David.

"It was an honor, Sir."

"Cut the shit Rogers. I don't plan on dying. I'm just taking as many of them out as possible, now go!"

They were in an abandoned warehouse on Laight Street, below Canal Street. The Blades had infiltrated the top floors and were entering the ground floor. Rogers stepped away and gave his men the orders.

"Sitrep Rogers." said David.

"All enemy personnel are in the building."

"Excellent. Then it's time to die. Make sure your men are clear. You have thirty seconds." said David.

Thirty seconds later David set off a detonation that imploded a quarter of the block.

Chapter Forty Eight

Getting shot hurts.

It hurts, but it's easy and usually involves small pieces of metal travelling at high velocity ranging anywhere from 700 to 1500 feet per second, and punching their way through you.

Letting yourself be shot is difficult, since that involves remaining still while someone else is doing the shooting. Every cell in your body is screaming for you to move! And you don't.

Except that John did. It was one of the first techniques Nakamura Sensei taught him and the hardest to learn. He called it multi-level blurring and it allowed you to avoid serious harm to internal organs. To blur while appearing to stand still was a very specialized ability. It meant that John would have to be moving just slow enough to let the bullet hit him while blurring fast enough to avoid serious internal damage, all while standing still and appearing to be shot.

The bullet tore through his left pectoral muscle and would have removed a large chunk of his heart had he not blurred. The surface wound was very real, so were the blood and the pain. As he fell to his knees, Trevor stood over his body. He knew he was going to pass out, loss of blood and multi-level blurring pushed him beyond his body's level of endurance. Trevor placed a foot on his shoulder and shoved him back as the world tilted, blackness filling the edges.

"You should have killed me when you had the chance, John," said Trevor as he pushed Mikaela into the car and drove off.

John opened his eyes in a bright room; the pain embraced him immediately. A hand on his shoulder pushed him back down into the bed.

"You need rest. I don't know how you did what you did. You should be dead right now." It was Masami.

"Where are we?" said John.

"The dojo, It was the safest and closest option." said Masami.

Lea walked in several minutes later.

"It appears you are very difficult to kill." said Lea.

"I hope you never have to find out how difficult." said John mid grunt as Masami pushed him back down.

"Where is the Sensei?" said John.

"The toxin –" Lea looked away.

"The toxin was too much for his system to take, even with my help. He went peacefully." said Masami.

The anger began to burn within John.

"He left you a letter." said Lea as she handed John a folded piece of paper. He took the letter and unfolded it.

Kane-San I write this letter because my time is short. I have lived a full life and have no regrets. You must find a woman named Rukio. After some investigation with my sources, I believe this is the person who began to instruct Kei. I believe she is the key. At the very least she can lead you to your Sensei.

You must master at least another technique. I am certain by now you know that there are five. Have Lea introduce you to her uncle Hideki.

Regarding Lea, I entrust her safety to your watchful eye. She can be impulsive and headstrong and I fear these events will cloud her judgment.

Be careful in whom you place trust. Find those who wish you harm and deal with them as lightning hits the ground – swiftly, decisively and with overwhelming force.

Himara

John folded the paper and remained silent for a moment.

"How do we find these bastards?" said Lea.

Lea was beside John's bed. John ignored Lea for the moment and turned to Masami.

"How long have I been out?" said John.

"An hour, I was able to get to you as soon as Trevor took Mikaela and left. I healed you first and then aided the woman." said Masami.

"What woman?" said John.

"Me." said Helen as she walked into the room. John had forgotten about Helen

"John, meet Helen Martine. Helen, John Kane." said Masami.

"Vest?" said John. Helen nodded.

"Re-kev or at least that's what David called it. It's stronger than Kevlar but reformed to be as light as a t-shirt. Something about interweave technology. In any case I'm glad I wore it." said Helen.

"I'm pretty sure that's the only reason you are still here to talk about it." said John.

"So you're Kane, huh?" said Helen.

"In the flesh." said John.

"I heard you took a bullet in the heart. Why aren't you dead?" said Helen.

"Masami there is very good with her hands." said John.

Helen didn't look convinced but didn't press the subject.

John winced as he sat up a little higher, looked at Lea and changed the subject.

"Lea, this is how we will find them," said John as he pointed at Helen.

"Can you still track whatever bug Mikaela put in my computer?" said John.

"How did you – never mind, yes I can." said Helen.

"Good let's find out who Trevor is working for. Masami, can I have my phone. We are going to need a car." said John.

"I have my Rover outside." said Helen.

158

"I appreciate the offer but I prefer something a little more secure."

John pressed the number that dialed Mole.

"Holy shit John! Your vitals were flat an hour ago and here you are calling me!" said Mole.

"Mole –"

"John what the hell – what happened?"

"Take a breath, Mole. How do you know about my – never mind, explain it to me later. I need a vehicle, something as close to a tank as Iris can get."

"What about the other vehicle?" said Mole.

"Taken, along with Mikaela." said John.

"What! Holy hell John. Details, later. Iris will be pissed but she'll understand. How soon do you need this?" asked Mole.

"Now." said John.

"On it, give me ten minutes." Mole hung up.

"How is CATT involved in this?" said Helen. "Why take Mikaela?"

Helen looked at John for a moment before he answered.

"It isn't." said John.

"Excuse me?" said Helen.

"CATT has been compromised internally. There are KO's – kill orders on Mikaela and David – Director Soros. That was Trevor's doing he needed access to the top. Somehow I feel we aren't seeing all of it. It seems like CATT is just part of it, a piece in a larger puzzle." said John.

John sat back a moment as he thought.

"Who stands to gain with those two out of the way?" said John.

"Don't know. I don't know the internals of CATT. I was just assigned to Mikaela." said Helen.

"By David I'm guessing." said John. Helen nodded.

"You were meant to be a huge wrench in the machine, an unknown variable." said John.

"I let my partner get taken. David is probably dead. I don't see me affecting much at the moment." said Helen.

"At the moment, Trevor thinks we are both out of the game. He's a smug bastard with an ego the size of Manhattan. It makes him sloppy. I'm more concerned about who is pulling his strings." said John.

Chapter Forty Nine

Trevor pulled up to an abandoned warehouse in Long Island City. Further in, from the hub of business and activity, there were still many old properties that were vacant. Trevor pulled the car into one of these and turned off the motor.

"Out." he said to Mikaela.

As they stepped out of the vehicle, they were immediately surrounded by Shadow Blades.

The Kage stood on a stairway and looked down at Trevor.

"As you requested," said Trevor pushing Mikaela forward.

"I have gone through some expense and trouble to destroy your little organization Mrs. Petrovich. Would you like to know why, before you die?" said Kage.

"You need the tech. The items that no one knows about or will admit exist. Starting with the nextgen surveillance system being put in place without anyone knowing." said Mikaela.

Kage smiled.

"Your intellect is indeed formidable. The reports about you have not been exaggerated. I am pleased. Please put her somewhere safe while we wait for our guests." said Kage.

"What guests?" said Trevor.

The Blades looked at Trevor, and began reaching for their swords. Kage raised a hand and they remained motionless.

"John Kane, Helen Martine and a special guest just for you, Trevor." said Kage.

"Impossible. I shot them both. They're both dead."

"Your ego will be your undoing." said Kage. "They should be here soon, prepare."

The Blades vanished from sight.

Chapter Fifty

Rukio looked down at the warehouse from several blocks away. It looked deserted unless you knew what to look for. The locks were new. Every fifteen minutes a "vagrant" would walk around the property. He looked homeless but he was too attentive. His gait told her he wasn't just a homeless person wandering the streets, he was well trained. This place was being watched and protected for a reason. She needed to know if that reason had to do with her purpose. She received the call earlier, confirming that her target, the one who caused her Sensei's death would be inside, tonight.

Tonight, the man she had been hunting would be within her grasp. Tonight was the last night of Trevor James.

John stood outside of the dojo as an H3 pulled up to the curb. A not too pleased Iris stepped out of the driver side. Behind the Hummer, a black Mercedes SUV G40 idled. John could count at least three in the Mercedes.

"Hello Iris." said John.

"John." she said as she nodded at the Hummer. "Short of bringing you an M1 Abrams, this is the best on short notice."

"Thank you Iris. Would it be possible to track the Phaeton?"

"We know where our vehicles are at all times, John."
She pulled out her phone and pressed the screen a
few times.

"As of thirty seconds ago, it is sitting at this
location." She showed the screen to John. "Do you know
where this is?"

"Yes, Queens LIC, a lot of industrial properties
there." said John.

"Good then I won't have to escort you there."

"Sorry about the Phaeton." said John.

"We'll get it back, one way or another." Iris
shrugged.

"In any case, thank you for the tank."

"Only for you, anyone else would have been cut off.
Mole and I will work out the details." she said as she
walked to the Mercedes. She tossed the keys to John
before she got in.

"Try not to lose this one, ok?" said Iris.

"No guarantees.' said John as he walked over to the
vehicle. The G40 reversed, swerved and sped away as it
changed direction leaving the way it had come.

John nodded as she drove away. Helen and Lea
joined John on the sidewalk. Knowing the car's location
meant he could confirm its position with the tracker
Mikaela placed on his computer. He turned to Lea about
to convince her to stay behind when Masami joined them
and gave him a slight shake of her head. He knew better
than to argue but felt he had to say something.

"This is going to get dicey. I know each of you have
reasons for coming." They all stared at him.

"I won't insult you by asking you to remain behind; I
know you are all warriors in your own right. I just want
you to go in with your eyes open. Are we all ready?" said
John.

They each entered the Hummer leaving John outside.

"I'm going to guess that's a yes." he said to himself as he jumped into the passenger side.

"Just tell me where we're going so I can get my partner back." said Helen.

John told her the address and she pulled off.

The drive to Queens from Brooklyn was quiet. John didn't expect conversation. It was Helen who spoke first.

"What kind of opposition are we facing here?"

Masami answered before John could.

"There will be Shadow Blades, many of them. Do not allow yourself to be cut. That would be lethal."

"Shadow Blades, I'm guessing are the guys in all black handling the short swords." said Helen.

"Yes they can be very dangerous, especially in great numbers. Death means nothing to them." said Masami.

"There are very few things a bullet can't handle." Helen said as she snuck a glance at John.

Masami nodded then added, "Make sure it's a head shot."

"Shit." hissed Helen.

"What?" said John.

"We have a tail." said Helen.

"How close to the location are we?" said John.

"About twenty minutes away. How did they even know it was us?" said Helen.

"I will be asking that myself, but I have a few guesses." said John.

"Let him tail us. I think this is more to make sure we don't deviate from a set course." said John.

"So what are we going to do? Just let them just follow us?" said Helen, anger creeping into her voice.

"Of course not, we, meaning you three, will keep going. I am going to deviate." said John.

As they turned a corner, John opened the door and blurred into the street, and began running. After half a

163

block he saw what he was looking for, a loading dock with a raised lip that would give him access to a low roof. From there he began to make his way to the warehouse on the rooftops.

Rukio saw the truck being tailed and then she saw someone jump out and blur. *Could it be possible? Could it be John?* This complicated things. She made her way to the target warehouse by rooftops. It was direct and circumvented the ground security. As she made her way to a raised ledge on the building adjacent the warehouse, a figure appeared on the opposite side of the same roof. Apparently she wasn't the only one who thought this approach worked.

"Hello John," she said without turning around.

She was aware that several people were closing in on their position.

"Rukio, I saw you die." The pain in his voice was evident.

"That was the plan. Sensei said he wanted you out of the life before it was too late."

She turned to face him. Her face was covered in white makeup. It was a traditional death mask. He noticed she wore the death robes as well, a brocaded garment of red silk. Two swords were strapped to her back.

"That was Sensei's idea?" he said.

She nodded mentally preparing herself.

"Are you planning on dying here tonight?" he said pointing at her clothing.

"I am always ready, are you? Why are you here, John?" she asked.

He had wondered the same thing and it always came back to Trevor and betrayal.

"I need to set things right. I need to deal with Trevor. Before this gets crazy and I don't have the opportunity, where is Sensei?"

Rukio debated lying for a moment.

"He is dead."

"Sensei is alive, Rukio." said John.

She didn't know that Nakamura Sensei was still alive the shock registered on her face briefly.

"How do you know this? This is a lie Sensei is dead" said Rukio

"If that's true then who killed him? Did you see him die like I saw you die?" said John.

"Who? Trevor or those he works for. Does it matter? The end result is the same. Sensei is gone. It is why I am here I will have my answers. I will kill Trevor and then I too will disappear. Do not stand against me John." she said.

"Rukio, no the Sensei-" began John. She cut him off with a look.

"John, there is nothing to say. Anything that could have been said never was." said Rukio.

"You know my feelings for you."

The words escaped his lips and hung there, alone.

"I can't be a part of your life, of anyone's life." she said.

She vaulted from the ledge onto the back of one of the Blades that had made it onto the roof, shattering his spine.

It seemed the Blades were focusing on Rukio. John counted seven, well six. One lay on the ground either paralyzed for life or dead. For a Blade, the latter would follow the former in short order.

John took a moment to watch her move. She had a dancer's body, agile lines and hard. He could see her move, the efficiency of each strike – no wasted

165

movement. It was beautiful and horrifying. John realized early the Blades stood no chance. *So what was the point of this attack?* he thought.

He scanned the rooftops and standing on the roof of an adjacent warehouse stood an observer hidden in shadow. Someone wanted to gauge Rukio's level of skill.

Using precise nerve strikes, she effectively neutralized the remaining six Blades. With the exception of the first Blade, this could have been a training exercise. John knew that Rukio's precision was enough of a message. The man on the roof stepped deeper into the shadows and disappeared from sight.

In that moment John knew, he knew she was better than he was. Rukio walked over to him then. No words were necessary as he looked into her eyes. The death mask she wore created a barrier stronger than any wall.

"If you get out of this in one piece," she said as she reached into her robes and placed a small book in his hand, "Find him – he can and will help you."

John looked at the slim notepad. Inside the front cover in precise handwriting it had a name and an address. When he looked up again, she was gone.

Chapter Fifty-One

John was running for the stairs when he heard what sounded like an explosion of tearing metal. Helen had opted leading her tail in the most direct route to the warehouse and drove the Hummer through the loading dock door.

Iris would not be pleased Several Blades approached the Hummer, only to discover it empty. Moments later the vehicle detonated rocking the building. It seemed Helen was resourceful. *If he made it through the night he would have to buy Iris a Hummer.*

The Blades could not pinpoint the threat. Those not killed in the blast began to regroup. As John descended the stairs, he noticed how quickly they reoriented. It took a high level of skill and combat training to react with that precision, in a matter of seconds. *Who the hell were these Shadow Blades?* The smoke, dust and debris made navigating the space almost impossible. In the midst of the chaos, John heard a voice.

"The assassin is to have her vengeance before she dies. The others are irrelevant. Kill them."

John jumped down to the balcony below.

"Mr. Kane. Glad you could join us." said Kage.

"And you are?" said John.

He recognized him as Takashi Fujita's killer, Kage.

"Going to kill you." said Kage.

Something about the self-assured manner, the quiet confidence in his answer set John on edge.

This man is dangerous, thought John.

John could see that it was just the two of them. Whoever he had been speaking to was no longer on the balcony with them. The man stood absolutely still. He gave John a slight bow and vanished.

"You are slow old man." The voice came from behind him. This was blurring on a level John had never seen.

"Your sensei was weak. In the end he did the only honorable thing." the disembodied voice said. "When faced with a superior opponent." the voice continued.

"Is that what you do, you go around killing old men?" said John.

"I do what I must. They are honored to die by my hand." said Kage's voice.

John could not locate a source, it seemed like it was coming from everywhere at once.

"The weak must fall; it is the natural order of things." said Kage.

Kage appeared before John and drove a palm heel towards his chest. The impact of such a strike would cause fatal internal damage. John managed to shift at the last second taking the strike on the right shoulder. His arm exploded in pain. A sharp intake of breath and the metallic taste of blood in his mouth told John things were bad.

John crashed into the door of an adjoining office, stumbling into an empty room, lined with windows but no other exits, a dead end.

"There's nowhere to go John, accept that and this will be easier." said Kage.

"Not dying here." said John to himself between gasps.

The pain was blinding as he shifted to meet the next attack.

"I would say that's being optimistic in the extreme." Kage said as he stood at the doorway. As he launched himself at John, the left wall of windows shattered.

Chapter Fifty-Two

Trevor stood in the epicenter of the chaos and destruction. He was trained enough to know things were only going to get worse before they got better. The best course of action would be to put two in Mikaela and disappear. *That is a good plan* he thought as he drew his gun.

"Now where would they have put her?" he said to himself.

"Hello Trevor."

The voice was like a knife sliding into the bone. It froze Trevor in place. As he turned, he fired. He was fast.

She was faster. She stood off to his left, in his blind spot. He knew she was there waiting for him to make a move.

"Hello Rukio, it seems the reports of your death are greatly exaggerated." he said without turning this time.

"It seems someone wants you out of the equation, Trevor." said Rukio.

"Do tell." said Trevor.

He didn't think he would meet death today. As he turned slowly to face her, he dropped the gun knowing how futile it was.

"How do you think I found you?" she said.

"That is an interesting question, one I'm afraid I don't have the answer to." said Trevor. "How is your Sensei by the way?"

"Dead." said Rukio. "Who ordered it?"

"An order like that would be above me. Give me some time I can make some calls, check my sources." said Trevor.

"A name Trevor or I am going to kill you slowly." said Rukio.

"You don't know what you're asking, what you are getting into!" said Trevor.

"The name." said Rukio as she blurred behind him holding a sword to his throat.

"All right, all right an order like that would have to come from the family heads, Ikken, Ikken Hisatsu." said Trevor

"Impossible," said Rukio.

"What do I gain from lying? Go and check. I guarantee you won't find him." said Trevor.

"Ikken Hisatsu is not a person, but it does explain much. Good bye Trevor." said Rukio.

Trevor was prepared for this contingency. It was an occupational hazard. He expected it sooner or later. He just didn't expect Rukio here now. It could only have been Kage. This was his version of wrapping up loose ends.

"Rukio, don't be foolish. Killing me will accomplish —" he began.

"Nothing, I know." she whispered into his ear. She buried the second sword she carried in his chest, puncturing his lungs and heart.

"This death is too good for you Trevor. And you are wrong. It serves one purpose: balance. Balance for the sensei, balance for me." said Rukio.

She removed the sword from his body in a way that would cause the most damage, slicing through his body. Trevor began to say something but his throat filled with blood and impeded any airflow. He was dead by the time he hit the floor.

Chapter Fifty-Three

Helen was glad she had talked Mikaela into the portable RFID device. It was a short range version given its size, but it worked perfectly within fifty yards. She found the room where Mikaela was held. It was lightly guarded by two Blades at the end of a corridor, on the other side of the warehouse.

It would have to be a silent kill since she didn't know if there were more Blades inside that would hurt or kill her partner at the slightest sound of a rescue.

She guessed the distance to be about sixty feet. Pulling out two knives, she took a few quick breaths, looked quickly around the corner and prepared herself.

"Fuck it." she said as she rounded the corner at the dead run. She threw both knives at the Blades trying to unholster their weapons. One knife buried itself in the Blades eye, killing him instantly. The other found its target in the left hand Blades' throat; he fell to the ground, clutching at his neck, futilely trying to stop the flow of blood. They were the last actions of a dead man. Helen looked down at the bodies as she withdrew her weapons.

"Bringing a gun to a knife fight – stupid." she said.

She opened the door slowly, ducking her head in and out quickly to draw fire in case someone was waiting for her. No response. She pushed open the door with her foot while remaining out of sight. Nothing, there was no motion or sound in the room.

She crouched low and rolled in the room to find a battered and bleeding Mikaela and two more dead Blades. Helen smiled in admiration as she picked up the unconscious Mikaela.

"Good job," she said more to herself.

Mikaela grunted as she was lifted. Helen could tell from the wounds that Mikaela needed medical attention. It was time to go. She almost crashed into a woman in the corridor. Helen instantly had her gun in her hand. Noise no longer an issue.

"Who the hell are you?" said Helen.

She noticed the two swords, one in the woman's hand and one strapped to her back. The one in her hand was bloody.

The woman came to a stop. She sheathed her sword slowly.

"My name is Rukio. You need help or she won't make it." Rukio said pointing with her chin

Helen couldn't see the woman's face behind the white mask she wore, she knew she was right: Mikaela needed help.

An interminable moment passed as Helen weighed if this woman was a threat.

"Fine, don't give me a reason to end you." said Helen. Rukio bent down and pulled out some supplies from her pack. She gestured to the room

171

"Let's go in there, out of this corridor." said Rukio. "Bring those bodies in here too."

Rukio looked at the two Blades by the door. Helen cursed herself for not thinking of that – it was a rookie move. Helen put Mikaela down as gently as she could and pulled in the two Blades. Rukio went to work dressing Mikaela's wounds. When she was done, Helen checked the dressings.

"Not bad. What do you want?" said Helen.

"I need you to deliver a message for me."

"A message to who?" said Helen.

"John. John Kane." said Rukio.

"You have my attention." said Helen.

"Tell him this goes beyond the Kage. He has to look at the Heads. Tell him to look for Ikken Hisatsu."

"For who?" said Helen.

"Could you repeat the message please? It is very important he gets it correctly." said Rukio.

Helen repeated the message without error. Rukio gave her a short nod and stood to leave.

"I'm sure I will see you again. Please take care of your friend." said Rukio.

With that she ran out the door and headed down the corridor, without making a sound. Helen lifted Mikaela, careful not to cause her wounds to reopen and made her way to the door at the other end of the corridor, marked exit.

Chapter Fifty Four

Lea and Masami crashed into the office. Masami quickly grabbed John's arm. The pain subsided instantly.

"Masami, you are only prolonging the inevitable." said Kage.

Masami's face was unreadable as she stepped forward to face Kage.

172

"You are so eager to throw your life away?" said Kage.

Masami remained silent but stood between John and Kage.

Lea grabbed John and began pulling him to a corner. Kage gave no indication he noticed the movement.

"Very well Masami, mistress life giver, let's end this." Kage said as he drew into a fighting stance.

He blurred and Masami reached behind her, placing a palm on his chest. A look of shock and rage crossed his face before he composed himself.

"Well done." he said as he massaged the muscle of his left pectoral where the blow landed. He blurred again drawing his short sword as he cut her abdomen. His cut was not as deep as it could have been, but the damage was done.

The poison coursed through her body. As she slid back, she allowed the poison to flow through her body. She absorbed the poison letting it course through her body. She controlled its flow reversing it and concentrated it in her hand.

Masami placed her hand on Kage's back allowing the poison to flow freely, giving him a massive dose. Then she fell to one knee holding her midsection. He meant to disembowel her and nearly succeeded.

"Is that the extent of your ability? Are you just going to reach out and pat me on the back?" he said.

He began to laugh and stopped short pointing his sword at her.

"You are pathetic and deserve to die." he spat on her as he raised his sword for the killing blow.

As he brought his sword down, he began to cough. He placed his hand over his mouth and blood covered the back of his palm when he pulled it away.

"What did you do?" he demanded.

Masami was breathing shallow now. Her face was covered in sweat. The poison burned her from the inside out.

"Death's Hand." she said in between breaths.

"That is a myth! A story invented by my grandfather to scare us!" yelled Kage.

Fear crept into his voice now.

"A life giver must also be a life taker." she whispered as she lost consciousness.

"No." Kage said more to himself as the realization dawned on him. "No, No!" He raised his sword and brought it down to strike Masami. The blow never reached her. John had intercepted the killing blow and placed a blurred palm on Kage's chest sending shockwaves through his body, destroying the muscle tissue of the heart and causing a complete loss of cohesion, disintegrating it. Kage slumped to the ground lifeless.

"John! We need to go now!" Lea was over Masami's body.

"Is she –?" asked Lea.

"No, but she will be soon if we don't get out of here." said John.

Now that he was able to take a moment, he saw that Lea was covered in small cuts and lacerations.

"Are you ok?" said John.

"It wasn't a cakewalk to get to you, but she did most of the fighting. Not since Sensei –" Her voice caught then.

"I know." said John as he placed a hand on her shoulder.

Lea recovered quickly.

"She is an amazing warrior. I would not want to face her in combat." said Lea.

John nodded, as he picked up Masami.

Her breathing was ragged and he feared for her life.

"Hang in there, Masami." John whispered.

As he walked out of the office, he saw the destruction caused by the Hummer, before and after the explosion. The Hummer itself was a burnt out husk. He could see where Trevor laid, his body placed against a wall, his face twisted in agony in the midst of the carnage. Rukio was nowhere to be seen but he knew she had been there. All around lay Blades dead or dying. John could see her handiwork as clearly as a signature. John headed down the stairs with Lea in tow.

"We need a way to get out of here before any authorities show up. We have five, maybe ten minutes at the outside." said Lea.

John was out of options. He doubted Iris would send him another car, considering he had just destroyed two of her vehicles. She was not going to be pleased. He found his cell phone and called Mole.

"John! Are you ok?" said Mole.

"I've been better. Listen Mole." he said quickly to cut off any further questioning.

"We need a ride and emergency med care."

"Shit John, Iris is going to be supremely pissed if you damaged her vehicles." said Mole.

"Three minutes Mole, then we are on the news." said John.

"OK give me three. I know a way Iris will agree to give you another car. No frills right. Just get from point A to point B right?" said Mole.

"Right point A to B." said an exhausted John.

"Ok see you in three, well two and a half. Leave the phone on." Mole hung up.

Before John could wonder what he meant by that last sentence, Helen stumbled in, holding Mikaela.

"She needs help now." said Helen.

175

"I have a ride coming soon. Will she make it? It will be two minutes." said John.

"She can but she needs real medical care soon. I don't know how much damage she took. Not my expertise, I'm usually the one doing the damage, not treating it." said Helen.

John understood, he felt as helpless with Masami. They made their way out of the warehouse through an exit to the rear. He hoped Mole would get someone there fast. He knew he could find him through the phone. It was one of the prearranged scenarios they had established. If John ever needed to be found in a hurry, he would leave his phone on and Mole would be able to pinpoint it within two feet.

John scanned the roofs of the building across the street. It was an old habit. Standing on the corner was the same man from earlier. He appeared to be waiting for someone. He bowed slightly to John, and then faded into the shadows.

"I think we need to put some distance between us and this place." said John.

John could hear the sirens in the distance, still a way off but getting closer. As he looked up the street, a van pulled up to them, screeching to a halt.

"Get in!" said the driver.

John knew it was Mole even though he had on a baseball cap and sunglasses. A bandana covered the lower half of his face. John opened the side door and Masami and Mikaela were placed in makeshift beds. Lea and Helen climbed in behind them. John rode shotgun.

"You look crazy with that on, you know." said John.

"Can't be too careful out here John, plus it was the only way I could get another vehicle. I had to personally guarantee it." said Mole.

176

"Thanks." said John.

"I live to serve." said Mole. "Now where are we going?"

"Furthest safe house from here with a med center." said John.

"I know which one. Ok buckle up!" said Mole.

As Mole pulled away, a series of explosions rocked the warehouse. John could see several fires starting on many of the floors. By the time the fire department arrived, it would be a full blown inferno. As he kept looking in the rear view mirror, a flash of red caught his eye. He could have sworn he saw Rukio walking away from the blazing warehouse.

"Wake me up when we get there, and take off that bandana. You're going to get pulled over." said John.

Mole took off the bandana but left on the rest of his disguise as he drove off, smiling.

Chapter Fifty Five

The implosion sounded like a muffled thump and was pretty quiet. It was the building collapsing afterwards that made the noise. Years ago the area below Canal, known as Tribeca, was an industrial wasteland. Now art galleries and designers had decided it was the new place to be. CATT had purchased the warehouse as an all-purpose storage facility. David had it rigged to collapse in the eventuality they needed to get rid of the sensitive materials inside.

It was never used as storage but the failsafe was functional. It was an implosion you could survive if you knew where to be, and which areas were meant to provide escape.

David, who had overseen the installation, knew. He extricated himself from the rubble slowly. One of the beams had bounced and gashed his left thigh. As he limped away, he heard footsteps behind him.

"That looks painful." said the figure still in the shadows.

"It's not too bad. And you are?"

"Here to end your life." David nodded.

"Mikaela?" said David.

"Alive and kicking, last I heard. That partner of hers is something."

David smiled. He knew having Helen with Mika was good.

"Will be a shame to eliminate her, but I do look forward to it." said the figure.

"You will find it much harder than you think." said David.

David had prepared for safety.

"Perhaps, but it is no longer your concern. Fast and painless or slow and painful, I was told to give you the choice." The man said this as he placed the silencer on a Glock 20.

"I prefer not to drag it out, Fa –"started David.

The whisper of the silenced death cut through the night, two shots in the forehead. The wounds blossomed as David fell to the ground. The assassin walked over and put two more into David's chest.

"I hope that was fast enough," he said as he walked off, into the night.

Chapter Fifty Six

The drive out to the safe house was long. Long because of the distance and long because of the route Mole took to avoid being followed. When they finally made it, the sun was high in the sky. John knew it had to be around just after dawn. As they pulled into the driveway, several people in scrubs greeted the van. John could tell they were at the Montauk property.

"I made a few calls ahead. They should be ok." said Mole.

"Thank you Mole." said John as the medical team carefully lifted Masami and Mikaela onto their respective stretchers and wheeled them into the basement of the house through the garage.

As safe houses went, this one was one of the most secure; one road leading to and away from the property. An eight foot wall surrounding the house proper and direct access to the ocean made it very hard to approach unnoticed, and easy to get away from.

The house itself was a fortress, with underground bunkers and reinforced walls and windows. It had its own power supply located beneath the property and enough food supplies to last six months. An extensive weapon cache was also located adjacent to the infirmary. This was a good choice.

"How long Mole?" said John.

"We have three, maybe four weeks. If we stay any longer, we need to scrap it." said Mole.

"Understood, get us ready to move in two weeks." said John.

"On it." said Mole.

Mole headed off making calls.

Lea and Helen made their way to the kitchen to get some food. John walked to the rear of the property. He was processing the events of the last few days and he did best thinking as he walked.

"Perimeter check?" It was Helen.

"Pretty safe out here for the moment, just thinking." said John.

"That reminds me, I have a message for you." said Helen.

179

"From who?" said John as he stopped walking.

"She was at the warehouse, white face, red silk and two blades, looking very dangerous, as in I wouldn't want to tangle with her. Ring a bell?" said Helen.

"Yes, yes it does. I wouldn't want to tangle with her either. What did she say?" said John.

"She said you need to look at the Heads. It goes beyond the Kage. She said to look for Ikken Hisatsu." said Helen.

John turned at the last sentence. Helen saw the expression on his face.

"That someone you know, this Ikken person?"

"Ikken Hissatsu is not a person." said John.

"That's what she said. Ok, what is it?"

"It means 'one blow, one kill," he said as the pieces started falling in place.

END

Thank you for reading Blur. I truly hope you enjoyed it as much as I enjoyed writing it. It was a great process, thank you for coming along for the ride. Please visit my blog, leave a comment and join my email list.

I look forward to hearing from you.

Other Books by Orlando Sanchez
The Spiritual Warriors

Connect with me online:
Blog: http://nascentnovels.com/
Facebook https://www.facebook.com/OSanchezAuthor
Twitter: https://twitter.com/SenseiOrlando

About the Author:

Author Orlando Sanchez has been writing ever since his teens when he was immersed in playing Dungeon and Dragons with his friends every weekend. An avid reader, his influences are too numerous to list here.

Aside from writing, his passion is the martial arts; he currently holds a 2nd Dan and 3rd Dan in two styles of Karate. If not training, he is studying some aspect of the martial arts or martial arts philosophy, or writing in his blog. For more information on the dojo he trains at please visit www.mkdkarate.com

Made in the USA
Middletown, DE
26 April 2019